**'You don't want to talk?' Nick asked, contrarily put out that she was going to ignore him. 'I thought this might be a good time to get better acquainted.'**

Annabelle turned towards him and raised dark, expressive eyebrows.

'We're going to be living together for the next two months, not to mention driving huge distances together and camping out together—don't you think we'll have enough time then to get acquainted?'

Annabelle wasn't sure why she was being so scratchy. Was it the shock of finding out that Nick Tempest was going to be her companion for the duration of the appointment?

Or the slightly uncomfortable feeling she'd always experienced in his presence?

Not that she knew him well—more by reputation than in person. But the reputation—playboy, womaniser, ambitious workaholic—made him the last person in the world she'd want to get to know. Not to mention the least likely person in the entire hospital—if not the planet—to be on this plane, heading for a two-month stint in the far Outback settlement of Murrawalla.

**Meredith Webber** says of herself, 'Some ten years ago, I read an article which suggested that Mills and Boon were looking for new Medical™ Romance authors. I had one of those "I can do that" moments, and gave it a try. What began as a challenge has become an obsession—though I do temper the "butt on seat" career of writing with dirty but healthy outdoor pursuits, fossicking through the Australian Outback in search of gold or opals. Having had some success in all of these endeavours, I now consider I've found the perfect lifestyle.'

### Recent titles by Meredith Webber:

SHEIKH, CHILDREN'S DOCTOR...HUSBAND
FAIRYTALE ON THE CHILDREN'S WARD*
BACHELOR ON THE BABY WARD*

*Christmas at Jimmie's*—duet

# TAMING
# DR TEMPEST

BY
MEREDITH WEBBER

First published in Great Britain 2011
Harlequin Mills & Boon Limited,
Eton House, 18-24 Paradise Road, Richmond, Surrey TW9 1SR

© Meredith Webber 2011

ISBN: 978 0 263 21893 0

Harlequin Mills & Boon policy is to use papers that are natural, renewable and recyclable products and made from wood grown in sustainable forests. The logging and manufacturing process conform to the legal environmental regulations of the country of origin.

Printed and bound in Great Britain
by CPI Antony Rowe, Chippenham, Wiltshire

**Praise for
Meredith Webber:**

A PREGNANT NURSE'S CHRISTMAS WISH

'Medical™ Romance favourite Meredith Webber
has written an outstanding romantic tale
that I devoured in a single sitting!
Moving, engrossing, romantic and absolutely
unputdownable. Ms Webber peppers her story
with plenty of drama, emotion and passion, and she
will keep her readers entranced until the final page.'
—*cataromance.com*

# CHAPTER ONE

ANNABELLE made the flight by the skin of her teeth. Kitty, who had volunteered to drive her to the airport, had insisted on taking 'shortcuts', so here she was, clutching an armful of carry-on bags, hurtling down the aisle towards the one vacant seat she could see right near the front of the small regional plane.

Fortunately it was an aisle seat so she could flop straight into it and stuff her belongings underneath before the flight attendant arrived to check her seat belt.

But the late arrival meant the plane was taxiing before she turned to look at her fellow-traveller.

To look, then look again...

'Dr—'

Typhoon, hurricane, cyclone—what in the name of glory was his real name?

'Tempest,' he said coolly, peering at her as if she were a complete stranger—maybe a patient he'd seen briefly in A and E. 'Nick Tempest.'

'Tempest, of course,' she mumbled hurriedly. 'I knew it was...'

She stopped before she made a bigger fool of herself,

but her agitation was growing. What was the man they called Storm doing on this flight?

Was there more than one possible answer?

Hardly!

'*You're* going to Murrawalla?'

She couldn't stop the question popping out, or hide the disbelief in her voice.

The plane lifted off the ground, the wings tilted, and it flew a wide, lazy arc over the city, but Annabelle barely noticed the houses growing smaller below her because as she looked past her companion towards the window, she discovered he was studying her.

Intently.

'Hang on, aren't you the new nursing sister? Been around for about four months? The one they call Belladonna?'

The hesitancy in his voice suggested he was far from certain it was her, but although Annabelle hated the nickname, she had to acknowledge he'd worked out who she was.

'It's Annabelle,' she said, turning so she could look into the blue eyes that had most of the female population of the hospital swooning every time he walked into a ward—blue eyes that had snared more than one man's share of female attention—or so the stories went. 'Annabelle Donne.'

'Ah!' He nodded to himself. 'I often wondered where it came from. You didn't strike me as being a walking, talking, deadly poison. More a target of some kind, I would have thought, from the number of times some sick child threw up all over you, or some drunk puked on your shoes.'

He wasn't smiling as he spoke so she took it as

criticism and was about to point out that someone had to look after the patients with stomach upsets when he spoke again.

'But you've cut off all your hair. That's why I didn't recognise you. No long schoolgirl plait trailing down your back, no tight little knot thing at the back of your head.'

Schoolgirl plait indeed, but, annoyed though the comment had made her, Annabelle could think of no suitable retort.

She made do with giving him a dirty look, though that didn't seem to faze him in the slightest.

He studied her for a moment longer, then said, 'Not that it doesn't suit you, but hair that length must have taken ages to grow, so why cut it all off?'

There was a surreal aspect to sitting in a plane high above the earth, having a relatively personal conversation about her hair—the loss of which she deeply regretted— with a man she barely knew.

And assumed she wouldn't like if she did know him...

Yet she found herself answering him.

'Have you ever smelt bore water?'

He frowned at her, but shook his head.

'It smells like rotten-egg gas and, as far as I've been able to discover, there's no shampoo yet made that can mask the smell. I did it as much for you—if you *are* the doctor heading for Murrawalla—as for myself. Travelling long distances in a car with someone who smells like bad eggs isn't pleasant.'

Nick Tempest stared at the woman in the seat beside him, a woman he knew yet didn't know. In the A and E department of the big city hospital where both of them had worked, he'd seen her as a calm, competent nurse, quietly spoken and so self-effacing he'd wondered if anyone knew her well. Because she hadn't been there long they hadn't shared many shifts, never working on the same team, so maybe his impressions were all wrong. What he did know was that she never shirked the dirty work some other nurses—and doctors—avoided, and that her gentle but firm manner with patients could nearly always avert trouble.

But that woman—the nurse—was very different to this slight but curvaceous woman in the seat beside him. Was it because she was wearing worn jeans and a slightly faded checked shirt instead of a uniform that for the first time he actually registered her as a woman?

Or was it the way her newly cropped hair clung to her head like a dark cap, accentuating the size of her brown eyes, the straight line of her nose and the curve of beautifully defined lips?

No, hair had nothing to do with lips.

Realising his thoughts had strayed into dangerous territory, he made his way carefully back to where this introspection had begun.

'You cut your hair off so it wouldn't smell?'

The lips he'd been trying to not look at curled into a teasing smile which, as a man who'd consigned all women to the 'only when needed' bin, he shouldn't have noticed at all, let alone registered as sexy.

Belladonna sexy?

More dangerous ground?

Definitely not! Lack of sleep, that was all it was. He'd been up half the night at the hospital, finishing reports and case-notes, and, naturally enough, though he'd not been on duty, answering calls for help when emergencies came in.

'Mostly for the smell but also the dust,' his companion was saying.

'Dust?'

This conversation was rapidly getting out of hand. He knew she was speaking English, so it couldn't be that parts of it were lost in translation, but—

'Bulldust,' she added, as if this explained everything.

In Nick's head it just added another level of confusion, and he was sorry he'd started the conversation, although politeness alone meant he'd had to say *something* to her.

'Is that an expletive? A slightly more proper form of bull—?' he heard himself ask.

This time she didn't smile, she laughed.

How long since he'd laughed?

Laughed out loud in that carefree way?

Relaxed to the extent that a laugh *could* be carefree?

'You've never been out in the bush before, have you?'

He heard this question, too, but was too distracted by the laughter—the laughing face of the woman beside him *and* his inner questions—to respond immediately. Besides, the captain of the flight was introducing himself and telling them when they were expected to arrive in Murrawingi, adding that the weather there was fine and warm, and he didn't expect any turbulence on the flight.

'Murrawingi?' Nick found himself repeating. 'I thought the place we were going to was called

Murrawalla. That's assuming, of course, you're the nurse half of the hospital team.'

'No airport at Murrawalla,' the nurse half explained. 'As far as I know, the pair we're replacing will take this plane back to Brisbane, leaving us the hospital vehicle to drive to Murrawalla.'

'Well, that's fairly stupid!' he muttered, annoyed he didn't know all these things—or perhaps annoyed that she did!

Or was he more unsettled than annoyed?

Unsettled?

Because he *didn't* know? Control had become important to him—he *did* know that!

Control had kept him on track when his world had imploded, Nellie ripping out his heart as casually as she'd—

Control!

But the pain he still felt in his chest when he thought of the baby was beyond control. No wonder he didn't laugh out loud these days.

'It's fairly stupid, having to drive to Murrawalla?' the woman queried.

'No,' he grumbled, clamping down on the pain, dismissing his unsettling thoughts and catching up with the conversation—reminding himself that he was looking to the future, not the past—and that he was heading west to learn. 'Calling places by nearly the same names.'

His companion smiled again.

'It happens all the time when aboriginal names are used. Further south, there's Muckadilla and Wallumbilla right next door to each other and both are fairly similar names so it's hard to remember if someone comes from one or the other.'

'Were you the geography whiz at school?' he asked, not because he wanted to know but for some perverse reason he wanted her to keep talking.

So he didn't have to think about the past?

Probably, but, for whatever reason, it was weird when he considered he tuned out a lot of the conversations going on around him without any problem.

Idle chatter irritated him—although had it always?

More questions buzzing in his head! No wonder he felt unsettled...

'Just well travelled,' Bel—no, he had to start thinking of her as Annabelle—said.

The attendant came through to ask if anyone wanted a newspaper or magazine, but although Nick said no, Annabelle took the morning paper.

'You don't want to talk?' he asked, contrarily put out that she was going to ignore him. 'I thought this might be a good time to get better acquainted.'

She turned towards him and raised dark, expressive eyebrows.

'We're going to be living together for the next two months, not to mention driving huge distances together and camping out together—don't you think we'll have enough time then to get acquainted?'

Annabelle wasn't sure why she was being so scratchy. Was it the shock of finding out that Nick Tempest was going to be her companion for the duration of the appointment?

Or the slightly uncomfortable feeling she'd always experienced in his presence?

Not that she knew him well—more by reputation than in person. But the reputation—playboy, womaniser, ambitious workaholic—made him the last person in the world she'd want to get to know, not to mention the least likely person in the entire hospital—if not the planet—to be on this plane, heading for a two-month stint in the far Outback settlement of Murrawalla.

The thought brought its own question.

'Why are you here anyway? When I had my briefing, Paul Watson was coming out for this term.'

Her companion—did she call him Storm or Nick? Dr Tempest?—smiled, but it wasn't a happy smile.

'Paul's girlfriend's pregnant and they've moved the wedding forward.'

'And you were the next bunny on the list?' Annabelle offered, certain there was no way this particular man would have volunteered.

But his next smile suggested she was wrong. It was positively smug.

'I volunteered.'

Annabelle just stared at him.

'Well, didn't you?' he demanded.

She nodded then added, 'But I had a reason—I wanted the extra bonus money.'

He sat further back in his seat, as if studying her from a distance might make things clearer.

'Well, well—monetary gain not dedication and self-sacrifice? I wouldn't have suspected that of you, Belladonna.'

'As you don't know me at all, you've no right to be making assumptions,' Annabelle snapped, really scratchy now as the man's arrogance shone through the sarcasm. 'And my name is Annabelle.'

He smiled as if glad he'd riled her, adding, with smarmy insincerity, 'Of course, that just slipped out.

Annabelle! Actually, it's quite a pretty name. Old-fashioned—'

'Reminds you of a cow,' Annabelle finished for him, sure he was going to add the tease she'd had to endure at high school.

But he surprised her by laughing, a low rumble of a chuckle that lit his eyes and made his rather harsh features soften.

'Don't be silly, we all know Christabelle's the cow. Annabelle's different—classy.'

Which left her with nothing to say, although maybe that didn't matter as Nick/Storm had turned away and was looking out the window at the whiteness of the clouds through which they were now flying.

Leaving her free to turn her attention to the paper, except...

'Why did *you* volunteer?'

She shouldn't have asked, she'd known that, but, well, *he'd* asked *her*...

This time his smile, as he turned, looked as if it had been drawn on his face and there was a suggestion of wariness in his eyes.

'Why would my reason be any different from yours?'

'Because you drive a Porsche and I drive a beat-up fifth-hand VW?'

It was too flippant an answer and as soon as the words were out she wished them back. As if it mattered what he drove! And hadn't she heard some story about the car?

A gift?

Surely not. Maybe a lottery win.

'I wouldn't have thought you were the kind of person who judged people by their possessions.'

The blue eyes were cold, and the drawn-on smile was gone.

'As you don't know me at all, you can hardly judge, but you're right,' she muttered. 'It's none of my business what you drive or why you're here.'

Hoping her cheeks hadn't coloured in embarrassment, she turned her attention to the paper.

The twinge of regret was so unexpected Nick didn't, at first, register it for what it was. He glanced at his companion, wondering if her concentration on the morning paper was pretence—a way out of an awkward situation.

Which *he* had caused with his cutting remark.

It didn't matter.

Better all round if they remained colleagues, not exactly distant but, well, professional.

Except that he'd admired the way she'd hit back at him, even if she'd coloured as she'd spoken and her voice had quavered slightly.

'Actually, I did have a valid reason,' he said, and she turned from the paper, her brown eyes widening so Nick was reminded of a small animal trapped in the headlights of a car at night.

'I'm officially on leave—accumulated holidays—but I'm taking over as head of the ER when I get back and it seemed to me that, in the new position, I shouldn't be choosing people for this outreach scheme when I didn't know the first thing about it.'

It wasn't the entire truth but it was a greater part of it. The other part—the idea that had been mooted—well, he'd have to wait and see, especially as Annabelle was speaking again.

'You could have visited for a few days, or a week,' she pointed out.

'And learned what? I'd have seen the place and maybe done a clinic or two but would that really educate me about the job I'm asking people to do?'

'No!'

But she frowned as she said it, studying him with questioning eyes.

His explanation had been so surprising Annabelle had no idea how to react. It was okay as far as it went—it *did* make sense for him to experience the placement—but trying to picture this man in a bush setting—*for two months*—impossible!

And there'd also been a pause in his explanation, as if he was holding back a little of it, though what it could be, and why he couldn't say it, she had no idea.

Fortunately, the attendant appeared, pushing a heavy trolley, offering breakfast trays to the passengers.

'They call this breakfast?' Nick—she was going to call him Nick—queried minutes later, eyeing with distaste the rather squashed croissant, pat of butter and tiny container of jam on his tray.

'There's juice as well,' Annabelle pointed out, reaching over to lift his sealed container of juice out of the coffee cup. 'And fruit.' She pointed to the square plastic container nestled in another corner of the tray.

'In fact,' she added, 'you can have my fruit and my juice. The croissant and coffee is enough for me.'

Nick barely considered her offer, suddenly struck by the truth of what she'd said earlier about the togetherness they'd share over the next two months. It was as if it had already started, with Annabelle offering him bits of her breakfast as naturally as a lover—or wife—might offer leftovers. Not that the act of offering bothered him— he'd eat her fruit—but the false intimacy of the offer made him feel extremely uncomfortable. Have mine—as though they were friends...

He ate his fruit and hers, drank both juices and had just asked for coffee rather than tea when the intimacy thing happened again. Not right away, but almost naturally...

'Two months still seems like overkill,' she said. 'If it's not the money, are you hiding out for some reason?' She must have realised how rude the question was for she lifted one dainty, slim-fingered hand and clapped it over her mouth. 'Don't answer that!' she added quickly. 'In fact, forget I asked. I'm not usually rude or inquisitive, it just seems strange...'

'Strange?' Nick echoed, wondering just what her impression of him was. His of her was fairly vague, good nurse who was always caught up in the worst situations in the A and E. 'Why strange?'

She turned towards him, a flake of croissant pastry clinging to her lower lip. Without conscious thought Nick reached out and wiped it away, then saw a blush rise beneath her skin as she scrubbed a paper napkin across her mouth in case any other scraps were lingering there.

It wasn't really intimacy, Nick told himself while Annabelle stumbled on in a kind of muddled explanatory kind of apology.

'Well, the impression of Nick St—Tempest... The impression the gossips pass on fast enough is of someone who has it made. Private schooling, smart car, great clothes, once married to one of the country's top models, always with a beautiful woman on your arm at hospital functions, easily mixing with the rich and famous, etcetera, etcetera, etcetera. I suppose that's why I was shocked to see you on the plane.'

Nick flinched at her summing up of him—did he really appear so shallow to his colleagues? Did no one suspect it was all a front—that the beautiful women were nothing more than armour? That since Nellie there was no way he'd ever open himself up to such hurt again? That work was his sole focus? His life?

Why would they?

He hid the flinch behind a half-smile and pushed her a little further.

'Never for a moment thinking it might have been pure altruism on my part? Doing my bit for the country?' he asked, and Annabelle laughed.

'Not for a nanosecond!' she agreed, smiling so broadly he was momentarily thrown off track. Though that hitch in his chest couldn't have had anything to do with this woman's smile!

'And,' she continued, 'you've already admitted it was a work-related decision, but doing it for two months still seems a bit excessive.'

He shrugged off the comment, unwilling to admit he was already regretting the impulse that had put him on this plane, especially since Annabelle had used the words *hiding out*. Now he considered this aspect of it, although he believed he was a man who could handle *any* situation, he had to admit there *was* an element of that in the decision, and a feeling of not exactly shame but something like it washed through him.

The hospital ball was coming up and he was tired

of finding someone to take to official functions—tired of explaining to the beautiful women that he wanted nothing more than a companion for the evening. But he knew from experience that not attending prompted more talk and speculation than him taking a different woman every time.

Added to which, Nellie was due in Brisbane for the annual fashion week later in the month and her face would be plastered on billboards and smiling out of newspapers and television screens, and try as he may to control it—control again—his stomach still clenched at the sight of that dazzling smile.

At the cold-blooded treachery it hid.

At the thought of what she'd done.

Control!

Fortunately the attendant was now pouring the coffee, so conversation could be forgotten.

He drank his coffee, looking out the window as he sipped, watching the broad ribbon of land unwind beneath him. Thinking of the past—not only of Nellie but of other losses—knowing it was time to put it all behind him and move forward. The challenge of the new job was just what he needed. He'd be too busy getting on top of that for the past to keep intruding.

Control!

But even as his mind wandered, his eyes still registered the scenery.

Every now and then the red turned green and he guessed at crops he didn't know the names of because he had no real idea what grew where, out here in what all Aussies, he included, called 'the bush'.

'See the huge dams?' Annabelle was leaning towards him, peering past him out the window, unaware her soft breast was pressing against his chest. 'They're for the cotton crops. They take more water out of our river systems than any other crop and it's causing problems for people further down the rivers and also slowly poisoning the whole river system.'

'You a greenie as well as a geography whiz?' he asked, finding, as she pressed a little closer, that her short, shiny hair diverted him from thoughts of soft breasts, smelling of lemons, not rotten eggs.

'Nope, but I think it's stupid to grow crops that need water in places that don't have all that much.'

'Like it's stupid for a man who doesn't need the bonus money to take this placement?'

She sat back and frowned at him.

'I didn't say that, and I sure as heck wouldn't criticise you coming out here for whatever reason you came. In fact, I'm really impressed to think you'd do it—to see it for yourself before sending people out. I was just surprised, that's all.'

But when she gave a little huff of laughter, Nick doubted she'd told the truth.

Until she explained…

'I was surprised to see you sitting there. In my mind you've always been the epitome of city-man. I mean, look at you. You're wearing suit trousers and a white shirt and a tie, for heaven's sake. And I bet there's a suit jacket stashed up there in the luggage compartment. You haven't got a clue.'

Nick felt a strange emotion wriggle around inside him and tried to identify it. He could hardly be feeling peeved—only women got peeved—yet if it wasn't peevishness squirming in his abdomen, it was mighty close…

'Do you insult everyone you meet or is this treatment reserved for the poor people who have to work closely with you?'

She laughed again.

'I'm sorry, it wasn't meant as an insult, just an observation.'

The laughter made him more peevish than before.

'Well, perhaps you'd like to keep any future observations to yourself,' he grumped, then he turned back to the window, determined not to speak to her for the rest of the journey.

Until he began to consider what she'd said to make him peevish. It had been about his clothes. His decision to come had been so last minute that he hadn't for a moment considered clothes, simply throwing most of his wardrobe into his suitcase—a wardrobe chosen mostly by Nellie, back when they'd been married.

Now words he'd learned from her—words like 'linen blend' and 'worsted', words like 'flat-pleated waist' and 'silk-knit polo'—came floating back to him.

He turned back to Belladonna, her true name forgotten in his horror.

'I've brought the wrong clothes. I didn't give it a damn thought, and I haven't a clue what a country doctor might wear, but you're right—it won't be a suit and white shirt. What do I do?'

To his relief she didn't laugh at him or say I told you so, but instead regarded him quite seriously.

'You'll have a pair of jeans in your case and a couple of polo shirts—you can make do with those.'

He shook his head. The one pair of jeans he'd taken into his marriage had been consigned to a charity shop by Nellie, who'd claimed he had the wrong-shaped butt for jeans.

And silk-knit polo shirts probably weren't what Annabelle had in mind for everyday wear in Murra-walla.

His companion frowned for a moment then shrugged.

'No matter. We can get you togged up in town—in Murrawingi—before we head west. There's a caravan park, which will have a laundry, so we can scruff everything up a bit before washing it and—'

'Scruff everything up a bit?' he echoed, feeling as if he was on a flight to Mars rather than the weekly flight to Murrawingi.

'You don't want that "new boy at school" look, do you?' his new wardrobe consultant demanded, and he shook his head, remembering only too clearly the insecurity stiff new clothes had produced when he'd first started at his private school, a scholarship kid from a different social stratum who'd known no one. Lonely but proud, he'd hidden his unhappiness from his classmates with a defiant aloofness, until he'd proved himself on the rugby field, gaining popularity through sport, his intelligence overlooked as an aberration of some kind.

Look forward, he reminded himself, turning his mind back to Annabelle.

'But I don't want to be spending money on new clothes either—especially clothes I'll probably never wear again.'

It was Annabelle's turn to shake her head.

'I know you mix in high society, but even there, good-quality country clothing is acceptable. Two pairs of moleskins, a couple of chambray or small-checked shirts, a pair of jeans and an Akubra. Actually, how big's your head?'

She checked his head. It was a nice head with a good bump at the back of it—not like some heads that went straight down at the back. And the silky black hair was well cut to reveal the shape.

You're talking hats, not heads, she reminded herself, wondering why she was so easily distracted by this man.

'My Akubra's a good size because I always had to tuck my hair into it, so it will probably fit you and, being a woman, I can wear a new Akubra without looking like a new chum.'

'I'm still back at the first mention of Akubra,' Nick admitted, looking more puzzled than ever. 'What the hell is an Akubra?'

Annabelle stared at him in disbelief.

'What planet do you inhabit?' she demanded. 'Surely there's no one in Australia, and possibly the world, who hasn't heard of Akubra hats?'

'Well, I haven't!'

He spoke stiffly and Annabelle realised he was embarrassed. A wave of sympathy for him washed over her and she reached out and patted his arm.

'I'm sorry. I won't tease you any more. You've obviously led a sheltered life.'

Sheltered? Nick wondered. As if! Although from the outside, looking in, he supposed people *would* assume that, especially people who didn't know how hard he'd had to work to reach his goals, or the sacrifices his parents had made to allow him to follow his dream.

He closed his mind on the past and turned his attention back to his companion. At least her chatter took his mind off things...

She had the paper open and was half smiling at whatever article she was reading. He wondered what she wanted the bonus money for—to spend on clothes, a man, an overseas holiday?

He had no idea, although he ruled out the man. His impression of her was that she was far too sensible—although without the hair she didn't look at all sensible. She looked pert and cute and kind of pretty in an unusual way, her high cheekbones too dominant for real prettiness but giving her an elfin look. Some middle European blood would be responsible for the cheekbones, he suspected, although her name, Annabelle Donne, couldn't be more plainly English.

'Why do you need the money?'

He hadn't intended asking her, but the fact that she was sitting there, calmly reading the paper, not the slightest bit interested in him now the wardrobe question had been sorted, had forced it out—more peevishness.

She closed the paper and folded it on her knee before turning to acknowledge she'd heard his question. Then she looked at him, dark eyes scanning his face, perhaps trying to read whether his question was out of genuine interest or simply a conversational gambit.

Whatever conclusion she reached, she did at least answer.

'I want it to pay my sister's HECS fees—you know, the higher education contribution for university studies. She's finishing her pre-med degree this year then going into medicine and I don't want her coming out burdened down by fees for the first few years of her career. I know people do it, and manage, but I can't help feeling those horror years as an intern and resident will be easier for her if she's not worrying all the time about money.'

'Your parents can't pay it?' Nick found himself asking, although *his* parents hadn't been able to pay, and the burden of debt *had* been hard in his early working years, especially once Nellie had come on the scene.

'My parents...'

She hesitated and he read sadness in her eyes and the droop of her lips.

They're dead, Nick thought, and I've just put my foot right in it.

'Our parents,' she began again, 'aren't always there for us. We're a mixed-up family but Kitty—Katherine— and I have a special bond so we've always looked out for each other.'

Which ended the conversation so abruptly he felt aggrieved again and slightly annoyed with her so it was easy to add other grievances, the clothes talk, the way she teased him, and now she was reading the paper again as if he didn't exist.

Well, he didn't have to like the woman with whom he'd be working for the next two months—just as long as they could work well together.

# CHAPTER TWO

HE CONCENTRATED on the scenery but unfortunately bits and pieces of what she'd been saying were rattling through his confused brain, taking him back to a much earlier conversation. What had she said? She'd been talking about bore water...

'Camping out together?'

The words exploded out of him, disbelief making them sound far louder than he'd intended.

It certainly got Annabelle's attention as she once again swivelled towards him, frowning now as she looked at him.

'What's wrong now?' she asked, with the kind of sigh that women used when they considered themselves faced with the inadequacies or stupidity of men.

'You said we'd be camping out together,' he reminded her. 'Earlier on when you were talking about your hair or my clothes or something. Why on earth will we be camping out together?'

No sigh but a smile in answer.

'Well, for a start, if you'd bothered to read the programme we were given, there's a B and S ball next weekend and then Blue Hills rodeo—or maybe it's a campdraft—the weekend after that, and although the

RFDS usually sends a plane and staff to those functions, we should still be there as it's an opportunity to get to know the locals. Then there's the—'

'Stop right there!' Nick held up his hand. 'Now, back up. Start with this B and S ball—is that like the bulldust you talked of?'

'You've never heard of a B and S ball?' She shook her head. 'Boy, you *have* led a sheltered life. B and S—bachelors and spinsters—is a country tradition. They're held at different cattle or sheep stations all over the continent—hundreds of people turn up and not all from the country. Some young city folk will do anything to wangle an invitation. It's also a bit of a ute convention as all the young men bring their utes and stand around comparing the modifications they've made to them— typical Aussie party, men in one group, women in the other.'

Nick was quite pleased that he didn't have to ask for an explanation of 'ute', his first vehicle having been an old utility he'd paid for himself, working at a fast-food outlet at weekends.

But he did need an explanation of why he'd be camping out at this festive occasion.

'Do we go to the ball for the same reason we go to the rodeo—to meet the locals?'

Annabelle's immediate reply was a dry chuckle, while her second wasn't any more enlightening.

'Wait and see,' she told him, and returned to reading the paper.

Nick turned back to the window. Below him the red-brown country seemed to stretch for ever, no green of crops now, just stunted grey blobs that must be small trees and a narrow tarred road leading directly west.

Every now and then he caught sight of a house, usually with a name painted in large letters on the roof.

Identification for the flying doctors? he wondered, but he didn't feel like displaying any more ignorance so he didn't ask Annabelle about the names.

The growl of the engines changed and flaps came down on the wings, the captain announced their imminent arrival and before Nick knew it they were on the ground.

'It'll be hot out there, and glary. You've got sunglasses?'

He nodded, although Annabelle wouldn't have seen this reply, too busy fishing under her seat for the bags she'd carried on board.

All around them people were standing and stretching, reaching into overhead luggage lockers, talking loudly now the journey was done.

'Where are they all going?' Nick asked, as Annabelle sat patiently in her seat, waiting for the jam in the aisle to ease before heading for the rear of the plane, where the only exit was.

'They're oil drillers and riggers coming back on shift,' she explained. 'You know one of the reasons the two Brisbane hospitals are doing this outreach project is that the town of Murrawalla grew almost overnight with the discovery of a new oil basin about sixty kilometres to the west. They're still drilling out there, and the men are flown in and out, two weeks on and two weeks off. There's accommodation on site, but no medical staff, and although the RFDS had always had a fortnightly clinic at Murrawalla, once you had the miners out there, it wasn't enough.'

'I knew about the drilling site, of course. I've spoken

to the CEO of the company, but I had no idea it was *sixty* kilometres away! Do we drive out there daily or just now and then?'

Annabelle stood up and gave him a look that suggested sarcasm didn't sit well with her.

'Whenever we're needed,' she said. 'It's the mining company that pays our bonuses, *and* contributes a large amount of money to the hospitals that supply staff, so don't forget that.' She led the way up the now all but empty aisle.

Outside it *was* hot—and this was winter? But the heat wasn't like the heat at home—this heat seemed to burn into the skin, drying it of moisture, making his eyes itch and his nose tingle.

He followed Annabelle towards a small tin shed that obviously did service as the air terminal, wondering how the hell he had got himself into this situation. Then she began to run, and training had him running right behind her, the suit jacket he held over his arm flapping against his body as he followed her.

He heard the sounds of chaos as he drew closer. Loud shouts and yelling, swearing that would make a policeman blush, thumps and thuds and the occasional cry of a woman. Inside the tin shed, a fight was well under way, rough, tough men hurling round arm punches at friends and enemies alike—or so it seemed.

Annabelle apparently had a destination in mind, so he followed her as she squirmed between the bodies towards a counter on one side of the building. Around them, figures lurched and dodged until, suddenly, one of the altercations was far too close to Annabelle. Nick thrust forward, putting himself between two battling men and the slight woman, using the bulk of his shoulders to protect her until he could lift her out of the way of the struggle and set her safely down behind the counter.

She looked up at him, and grinned.

'Sir Galahad?' she teased, and he doffed an imaginary hat and bowed in front of her.

'At your service, ma'am!'

It was a light-hearted exchange but Nick sensed a shift in the dynamics between them—a shift instinct warned him not to investigate…

In front of the counter, a man and woman were bent over a figure slumped on the floor.

'Let's see if we can get him up on the counter, take a look at him. If we leave him here, we'll all be trodden on,' Nick suggested.

The man glanced up.

'You the new doc?' he guessed, and the Nick nodded.

The man grinned at him. 'Welcome to the wild west. I'm Phil Jackson, departing nurse.'

Together they lifted the injured man onto the counter, as a lone policeman came in through the front door, whistle blowing shrilly in an attempt to calm the melee.

'This is Deb Hassett, the doc,' Phil said, introducing the woman by his side and standing back while Nick examined the injured man. Annabelle introduced herself and Nick then, as the fight began to settle down around them, she suggested she and Nick take care of the injured man while the other pair readied themselves for departure.

Phil shook his head.

'The plane won't go for a while. This fellow is the dispatcher—the guy who checks everyone's ticket and takes out the luggage and loads it on board. Guess the pilots will have to do it themselves now, so there'll be a delay.'

The man on the counter began to move, moaning piteously and squirming around on the hard counter.

'The bastard hit me,' he said, trying to sit up as if determined to find his attacker and continue the fight.

Nick was pressing his fingers into the man's jaw bone, already swelling beneath a red abrasion, feeling for any sign of movement that would indicate serious damage then continuing his exploration by pressing fingertips to his patient's cheekbone and eye socket.

'Everything seems to be intact,' Nick finally declared, helping the man sit up, which was when they all saw blood, leaking from the back of the man's head, pooled on the counter and soaked into his khaki shirt.

Annabelle headed for the bathroom, returning with a bunch of paper towels and her hat filled with water.

'I couldn't find another container,' she muttered, when she saw the look on Nick's face. 'And we only need it to clean up the blood so we can find the injury.'

She proceeded to mop at the man's head, seeking the source of what seemed like a massive haemorrhage but was probably only a freely bleeding scalp wound.

'And surely there's a first-aid box in this place,' she added, looking around for Phil or Deb, who might know where it would be.

'They went outside,' Nick told her, finding the cut on the man's head and pressing a wad of clean, dry paper towels to it.

He'd barely spoken when the pair reappeared, carrying what seemed like a large chest between them.

'Why we don't have small first-aid boxes in the

vehicle I don't know,' Phil complained as he opened the box then looked up at Nick. 'What do you need?'

'Razor to clear some hair, antiseptic, local anaesthetic then sutures.' He was on autopilot as far as tending the patient was concerned, so his mind was able to process a lot of other concerns. 'Why are we doing this? Murrawingi is a big enough town to have a clothing store, surely it has a hospital and doctor and even an ambulance.'

'You're right.' It was Deb who answered while Phil passed him a sterile pad soaked in brown antiseptic. 'But there was a bad road accident a hundred k south of town early this morning and the whole team's there.'

Phil nodded briefly towards the young policeman, now talking to the pilots from the plane.

'That's why we've only got the baby policeman here.'

'He seems to be doing a good job,' Annabelle said, feeling someone needed to defend the young man. 'I mean, the fight stopped, didn't it?'

'Jim, one of the drillers, stopped the fight. He's a big devil and he just lifted the bloke who started it up in his arms, carted him outside and told him to stay there until the plane was loaded. Not many people argue with Jim.'

Nick had just finished stitching the cut and was taping a dressing over it when the young policeman approached.

'Where's the dog?' he asked, and although Nick and Annabelle could only shake their heads, the other pair obviously knew all about a dog.

'That's him you can hear barking out the back,' Deb said. 'This fellow got the dog into the container before the other guy hit him. Said he had to weigh him and he crated him at the same time, then he snapped a lock and wouldn't give the other bloke the key so the dog's owner hit him.'

The young policeman looked bemused, and this time it was Phil who came to his rescue.

'We'd just checked our luggage in when it happened. Apparently the dog was booked to fly but as Henry Armstrong, travelling with Bill Armstrong, but when Henry turned out to be a dog, the clerk said he had to travel in a crate and Bill went berserk, insisting he'd paid for a seat and Henry had every right to sit in it.'

Annabelle was watching Nick as the story was revealed, watching the parade of emotions—mostly disbelief—passing across his face. But the question he finally asked was the last she'd expected.

'The dog's called Henry? Whatever happened to names like Spot and Rover?'

No one answered, the young policeman now intent on getting the passengers onto the plane, checking again with the pilots that they were willing to carry Bill Armstrong in spite of the trouble he'd caused.

'As long as he agrees the dog goes in the crate, we'll take him,' one of them said, then he turned to Deb. 'I don't suppose you could carry a tranquillising dart with you just in case?'

Deb laughed, but Annabelle suspected the pilot wasn't joking. No doubt he flew this route often and knew the rough, tough men he carried. Maybe it explained why a small plane on a country route had two pilots.

People were moving towards the doors leading out onto the tarmac.

'That's it?' Nick said to Phil. 'No one's going to

charge the fellow with assault? And what about our patient? Do we just leave him here, or take him to the hospital or what?'

'I'll take him up to the hospital when I've seen the plane off,' the young policeman offered, before leaving them to help a couple of volunteers carry the luggage out to the plane.

Phil and Nick eased the patient off the counter and settled him on a chair behind it, while Deb and Annabelle cleaned up the mess.

'Easier not to charge anyone,' Phil explained. 'If they booked someone every time there was a bit of a barney, they'd need a bigger jail and a full-time court sitting out here.'

He turned to Annabelle and dropped a bunch of keys into her hand.

'I've locked the chest. You guys'll take it back to the car? It's the old troopie with the bent snorkel, can't miss it, and Bruce'll need a run before you head out on the road.'

He took Deb by the arm and headed for the plane.

Annabelle hefted the keys in her hand, knowing they'd have to work out what they were all for—the car, the small hospital at Murrawalla where they'd be stationed, the house they'd share, and all the medical chests that held the necessities of their trade.

The house they'd share...

She was considering this aspect of the two months and wondering why the thought made her feel distinctly uncomfortable when she realised Nick was speaking to her.

'What the hell did he mean when he talked about a

troopie with a bent snorkel and who, do you suppose, is Bruce?'

Annabelle turned to look at him, seeing bloodstains on his white shirt and dark stains smeared across his trousers, indication that the blood had spread, and that he'd definitely need some new clothes.

'The troopie is our vehicle. It's a Toyota, I think built originally to carry troops, hence the name. It's one of the most uncomfortable four-wheel drives ever put on the road, but it will go anywhere with a minimum of fuss, which makes it ideal in this country.'

'And the bent snorkel?'

Annabelle smiled at him.

'I think the bend is accidental but when you see the snorkel you'll understand. It's like a snorkel you use when swimming, only a car one that takes the exhaust up over the top of the vehicle so if you're going through deep water it can't get into the exhaust pipe and cause the engine to overheat.'

Nick shook his head.

'After showing that level of ignorance, I hardly dare ask about Bruce.'

This time Annabelle laughed.

'Bruce, I imagine, is our dog.'

'*Our* dog?'

'Ours for the next two months!'

'I've got a dog called Bruce?'

'No, no,' Annabelle said, laughing so much she could hardly speak. '*We've* got a dog called Bruce!'

'Well, you'd better keep him under control,' Nick grumbled. 'Because there is no way in this world I'm going to stand around calling out Broo-ooce, or, worse still, Brucie, to any darned dog.'

He crossed the room to where their fellow passengers were retrieving luggage from a trolley and picked out a new-looking suitcase, then turned towards Annabelle.

'Which is yours?' he asked, but she was already reaching past him, swinging a battered backpack onto her back then lifting a bulky roll with a strap around it off the trolley.

'Swag,' she said, no doubt reading the question on his face before he'd even asked it. 'There'll be swags in the troopie as part of our equipment but I like to use my own.'

'I thought swags were what swagmen carried during the depression, a kind of bed roll.'

'Exactly,' Annabelle replied. 'They're back in vogue, you know. I doubt there's a young man anywhere west of the main cities who doesn't have a swag he can throw in the back of his ute.'

'Not only a foreign place but a foreign language,' Nick muttered to himself as he followed Annabelle out of the airport building. She appeared to be heading for a large, bulky-looking vehicle, custard yellow under a film of red dust. He studied it, seeking the snorkel, which he finally identified as a black pipe coming up alongside the driver's side windscreen, this particular snorkel bent crazily forward at the top.

Annabelle had stopped and was fiddling through the keys, although as he joined her she nodded towards the bent pipe.

'Backed it under a low branch I'd say, wouldn't you?'

Nick nodded in turn. He was too bemused by the strangeness—by the hot, dry air, the red dust already coating his shoes, this battered vehicle and an undoubtedly capable nurse—to make a comment on the driving skills of his predecessors.

Then a question he should have asked earlier occurred to him and he studied the capable nurse.

'How come you know all this country stuff?' he demanded, and though he expected a teasing smile and some light remark in reply she said nothing, just concentrated on the bunch of keys as if the large one that had 'Toyota' written on it hadn't already been singled out by her nimble fingers.

She unlocked the doors at the rear of the vehicle and threw her pack and swag into a narrow space between chests of medical equipment, large plastic containers of water and a small, chest-like refrigerator. Nick hoisted his suitcase and set it on top of another chest, then remembered they had to collect the one from the terminal.

'I'll get it,' he offered, but Annabelle followed him anyway, knowing it would be easier to carry if they shared the load.

And as she followed she considered the question she hadn't answered. How to explain that this was the country of her heart? Or that she'd volunteered not only for the bonus money but so she could come out here to face the past, and hopefully put it behind her, enabling her to move on, strong and confident, towards whatever the future might hold.

He'd have thought she'd lost her marbles, and the poor man was confused enough as it was.

She caught up with him and together they carried the chest out of the now-deserted terminal building. Back at the troopie, it was Nick who found where the chest went, behind the driver's seat and accessible only by tipping the seat forward.

The success must have gone to his head for next minute he was demanding the keys and settling himself into the driver's seat, man-confident there wasn't a vehicle made he couldn't drive.

Until he noticed the two gear sticks...

Annabelle smiled to herself as she climbed into the passenger seat and watched the frown deepen on his face as he tried to work it out.

'Okay,' he finally admitted, 'tell me!'

'One's for the four-wheel drive,' she said, pointing to the smaller of the two. 'You put the main one into neutral before engaging four-wheel drive and you have to lock the hubs on the front wheels.'

His frown was now directed right at her.

'And other city doctors who come out to this godforsaken place find this out how?'

'I guess they read the manual, or perhaps the information is passed on from the departing pair—there'd have been plenty of time for Phil to explain if it hadn't been for the fight.'

'Can you drive it?' Nick asked, and Annabelle nodded then watched him get out, walk around the bonnet and open the door on her side.

'It's all yours. I'll read the manual while we're travelling.'

She smiled at him as she slid back out to the ground.

'Well, at least you're not too stubborn to admit you don't know something. I could name half a dozen doctors in A and E back home who'd cut their tongues out before admitting a woman might know more about a vehicle than they did.'

Nick returned her smile with interest, flashing a gleaming grin alight with teasing self-mockery.

'My ego's taken such a battering already, one more blow is hardly noticeable.'

They swapped seats but it wasn't until Annabelle started the engine that she heard a short, sharp bark and remembered Bruce.

'Ha! You don't know how to drive it either,' Nick said, but she was already out of the vehicle, looking around her, finally locating the dog tied in the meagre shade of a gidgee tree at the edge of the car park.

'Bruce?' she called, and got an answering bark, but as she approached the dog she wondered just how adaptable he was to the medical staff who came and went from Murrawalla. He seemed to be largely blue cattle dog, a dog known to be loyal to one master, but Bruce's slavering, tail-wagging, stomach-crawling behaviour as she approached suggested he was happy to be in any human company.

She let him sniff her hand and, as he continued to greet her with grovelling wriggles and little whimpers of delight, she unhooked his lead from the tree, picked up the empty water bowl and led him back to the vehicle.

'That's not a dog, it's a small wolf,' Nick announced as the dog approached him, prepared to offer Nick as much love as he'd offered Annabelle. 'And just where does he sit? Not on my knee, I hope.'

But his attention to the dog, the way he scratched between his ears and under his chin, convinced Annabelle that he was all talk. Bruce had won him over in a matter of seconds.

Bruce settled the matter of where he would sit when Annabelle opened the back doors. The dog leapt in and dropped down onto a padded mat on top of one of the chests, his head against the luggage barrier that divided the front seats from the back part of the troopie. One glance at Bruce's favoured position was enough to convince Annabelle she'd drive as often as possible. Whoever sat in the passenger side was sure to get a good amount of Bruce's drool down the back of his or her neck.

They drove into town, Annabelle pulling up in front of the general store, which she knew from the past sold everything from groceries to underwear, from water tanks to televisions. Across the road a group of men sat on the low veranda of the local pub, cool in the shade of the wide eaves. They nodded their acknowledgement of a couple of strangers in town and returned to their drinking without comment, although Annabelle did wonder what they'd made of Nick in his bloodstained suit.

Once inside the store a keen young man took charge, checking Nick's size and producing a couple of pairs of moleskin trousers, a pair of jeans, and three shirts within minutes of their arrival, then hustling Nick towards a dressing room to try them all on.

Annabelle took the opportunity to try on the hats, finally settling on a neat black number with a good brim and the ability to tilt saucily down over one eye.

Could she afford it?

Not really, but it was a great hat and it really would be better for Nick to have her old one, rather than advertising his new chum status in a brand-new Akubra.

Although why she was worried about what people might think of Nick she wasn't sure.

Was it because she sensed a hint of vulnerability beneath his unyielding exterior, not just the uncertainty natural to a newcomer to the bush, but something deeper—some pain—hidden behind the hard polished surface of Nick—Storm—Tempest?

She tried tilting the hat to the other side and considered herself in the mirror, considering also why the man's vulnerability—imagined or otherwise—was any of her business. He was noted for his lack of commitment to the women he took out, while her one and only serious experience in the relationship department had been so disastrous she'd been forced to realise she had to start again, going back to the first man she'd loved—the first man who'd deserted her—her father.

Making her peace with him and the past so she could move forward...

# CHAPTER THREE

'WHAT do you think?'

Nick appeared from the dressing room, holding his arms wide so she could admire his new look.

Stunning, but she didn't say it, feeling slightly ill because her heart had given a little lurch when she'd seen how the blue shirt accentuated the blue of his eyes and the way the moleskins clung to his long legs.

'Well done,' she *did* say, speaking to the sales clerk, not Nick. 'Now all we have to do is rough them up a bit and he'll be ready to face Murrawalla.'

'I run my ute over my new clobber,' the young man offered, and Annabelle wished she'd had a camera to catch the stunned-mullet look on Nick's face.

'Make sure the zips and buttons are done up,' the salesman added, 'although they don't seem to suffer much damage—just sink into the dust.'

Nick made a kind of bleating noise, but was obviously still too bemused by this latest bush conversation to question it or protest, although he did make a token objection when Annabelle suggested he get back into his other clothes so all the new gear could be washed.

'And driven over by the troopie?' he managed. 'Is that acceptable, or does it have to be a ute?'

Annabelle laughed.

'We won't run over the shirts,' she told him kindly. 'The trousers will pick up enough dirt to spread through the wash and tone them down a bit. You're getting jeans as well? Boots?'

He stared at her and shook his head, but she knew he wasn't answering her question, just portraying disbelief at the situation in which he'd found himself.

The scruffing, washing and drying of the clothes took them another hour, but as Nick changed in the ablutions block at the caravan park, he knew it had all been a good idea. The trousers were great, comfortable to wear, softer now than when they'd been pristinely new. And they looked good, as did the shirt with the two pockets. In fact, as he tipped Annabelle's battered old hat into a rakish angle on his head and checked the mirror, he had to smile.

City-man, Annabelle had called him, but no one looking at him now would think that.

'Finished admiring yourself in there?'

'Is there a spyhole in the wall?' he answered, picking up his soiled clothes and coming out to join her and Bruce at the troopie, parked in the shade of a huge tree, with long drooping branches that reminded him of a weeping willow.

But he knew they grew along creeks and rivers and as there were no creeks or rivers within coo-ee of this place, he wasn't going to make a fool of himself by suggesting a name.

No, he'd work out how to drive the troopie, he'd lock and unlock wheel hubs and he'd never give Annabelle cause to call him city-man again.

Though why it mattered what she called him, he didn't know.

'I gave Bruce a run and filled up with fuel while you were watching your laundry dry,' she told him. 'I also got us some sandwiches to eat on the way and a couple of cans of soft drink as well. I have a feeling I should do a proper shop while we're here, because although Murrawalla has a roadhouse that sells groceries, meat, fruit and veggies, the prices will be much higher.'

She looked sufficiently worried about this dilemma for Nick to ask, 'Are we in a hurry that you'd prefer not to shop here?'

'Not really. We've a way to go, but the road's good. No, I'm more worried about not buying local. I mean, if everyone in Murrawalla—'

'All one hundred and forty of them,' Nick put in.

'Yes, but if they all shopped here in Murrawingi then the roadhouse would stop stocking even the basics and that's bad for their business but also for the town.'

Nick shook his head.

'I was just telling myself you'd never call me city-man again, but for someone who's used to corner stores and local supermarkets open twenty-four hours a day, this conversation is mind-boggling. However, I get your drift, we'll shop locally, and if it costs us a little more, too bad. Now, show me how to drive this beast and let's get going.'

Once he had the hang of the gears, he drove competently, Annabelle realised, but, then, he probably did everything competently, even expertly. His reputation as a doctor was that he was always thorough, always willing to go one step further with a patient if he suspected there might be hidden problems. It was only his social reputation—if one had such a thing—that had given her cause to wonder about him when she'd seen him on the plane.

Not that his social reputation was any of her business. She reached forward and turned on the two-way radio, tuning it so they could hear messages without the chat between truckies and farm workers overwhelming them.

'Do we use that?' Nick asked, indicating the handset.

'Only if we need to,' she told him. 'I don't think there's much point in just chatting to people. The truckies do it to keep themselves alert, but I imagine it's only in here for emergencies as far as we're concerned.'

'This is Eileen at Murrawalla hospital—is the doctor's car receiving? Are you new guys there?'

'You must have wished that on us,' Annabelle told Nick, lifting the handset to her lips and pressing the button to transmit.

'We're the new guys and we hear you,' she said, then switched to receive.

'Good! Where are you exactly? There's a problem out on Casuarina, if you tell me where you are I'll give directions.'

'We're only sixty kilometres from Murrawingi— slight problem at the airport,' Annabelle reported.

'Well, that still makes you the closest and at least you won't have to backtrack. About another fifteen k up the road you'll see a mailbox made out of an old bulldozer track, turn right there and follow the road another fifteen k to some cattle yards, turn left and about thirty k further down that road there's a bloke in trouble in a washout. When you're done you can follow that road—it

eventually leads back to the bitumen about twenty k
south of town. Casuarina is sending a tractor over to get
the truck out but he'll travel slow. Radio if you need the
ambulance as well.'

'A bloke in trouble in a washout?' Nick echoed, as
Annabelle checked the distances she'd written on a small
notebook she'd found bound to the sunshade by a thick
rubber band.

'Sounds like a single car accident,' she explained.
'This is channel country. It's dry now but when you
get good rain up north, the water travels south and this
area becomes a maze of small creeks that criss-cross
the whole area. Once off the bitumen you drive in and
out of these all the time, and some of them have steep
drop-offs at the bottom. There's the mailbox.'

Nick looked towards where she was pointing and was
amazed to see that the mailbox had indeed been fash-
ioned out of the track of an old bulldozer. He turned right
onto a narrow dirt road, making a note of the kilometres,
although he was fairly sure he'd recognise cattle yards
when he came to them.

'Better stop and lock the hubs just in case,' Annabelle
suggested, and he pulled up and watched as she walked
to the front wheel on her side, bending over to shift the
hub from free to lock. He went back to his side and did
the same thing.

'Are we now in four-wheel drive?' he asked, wondering about the next move.

She shook her head.

'No, but we can go into it if we need to now the hubs
are locked. We should lock them every so often whether
we're using the four-wheel drive or not, to keep them
lubricated.'

She passed him as she spoke and climbed into the driving seat.

'It's not that I don't trust your driving,' she said, 'but we should get to this guy as quickly as we can so it's not the ideal time to be starting your new driving lessons.'

Nick didn't argue, although as he climbed back into the troopie and felt Bruce's hot breath on his neck, he did feel entitled to a small grouch.

'It's a good thing I'm a modern man who isn't fazed by women's lib or the fact that one particular woman is outdoing me at every stage of this adventure.'

Annabelle turned towards him, as if startled by his admission, then she smiled.

'Not at every stage,' she reminded him. 'You did rescue me from being trampled back there in the airport.'

She smiled again, though Nick was starting to wish she wouldn't. She had such an attractive smile—the kind of smile that not only made you want to smile back but made you want to keep her smiling.

He shook his head, sure it had to be the heat—heat-stroke—that had his mind wandering this way.

Although the vehicle was air-conditioned...

'Hold on!'

The clipped order had him grabbing for the bar on the front dashboard, catching it just in time to stop himself being thrown forward against his seat belt.

'That's a washout,' Annabelle explained as she eased the troopie into its lowest gear so it had to growl and grumble its way out of the creek bed. 'I'm sorry, but going in it didn't look as steep as that. I'll take them all much more slowly in future.'

Still uncertain about the geography of it, Nick opened

his window and stuck his head out to have a look. Clouds of red dust whirled in, but behind them he could see what Annabelle had meant. The road had seemed to ease slowly into the cry creek bed, but at the bottom it had been cut away so the last two feet of the descent had been abrupt.

'Window up,' she ordered, putting the vehicle back into a higher gear. 'And now you've had your first taste of bulldust, maybe you'll keep it up in future. Not that having the windows shut keeps it out—the stuff gets in through every crack and crevice and infiltrates your body, food, clothes and hair. It's like a physical presence in your life, something you have to live with for the next two months.'

They reached the cattle yards, solid steel structures that lacked the romance of the old timber cattle yards Nick had seen in movies and had pictured in his mind.

'There are ants out here that could eat through timber stockyards in a week,' Annabelle told him when he queried this. 'The old-timers used a particular timber the ants wouldn't eat, but once those trees were all cut down, it was time to move on to steel.'

But although the explanation was clear and satisfactory, he knew most of her attention was now on the road, seeking out more traps for unwary drivers, looking ahead to what they might find at one particular washout.

It was a vehicle about the same size as the troopie, but with a tray back. Tipped on its side, it made a macabre picture, one that Nick could not make sense of no matter how hard he studied it.

'Roo shooter,' Annabelle said, stopping the troopie at the top of the incline leading down to the creek crossing and waiting until the dust settled before opening her door.

Now the scene made sense, the bodies strewn everywhere were the man's haul for the night. From what Nick could see, they'd been hung on racks above the tray of the big ute and had slewed in all directions or been flung off when the vehicle had tipped over.

He followed Annabelle down the slope, aware of the steepness and glad he'd had the sense to add a pair of strong, elastic-sided boots to his purchases. Their rubber-ridged grips made the journey a lot easier than it would have been in his city shoes, and the boots would get nicely scuffed scrambling down here.

Annabelle had reached the cabin of the ute and was trying to wrench open the door.

'Pinch bar in the toolbox on the back,' a faint voice said, and Nick peered past her to see the driver trapped behind the steering-wheel, but fortunately conscious. The handset of the two-way he'd used to call for help was still clenched firmly in one hand, the radio chattering on regardless of the drama being played out here.

*At least I know what a pinch bar is,* Nick thought, remembering all the times he'd gone on handyman jobs with his father. He climbed carefully up onto the cambered vehicle and was about to open what he guessed was the toolbox when a loud, threatening growl stopped him. In front of the box, in a cage fitted to the tray of the ute, was a huge dog, positively drooling in anticipation of biting Nick's head off.

'You're safe, he can't get at you,' Annabelle assured him, but Nick had already stopped worrying about the dog and was now worrying about the flies that had formed a thick black cloud around him and seemed intent on entering every orifice in his head.

Brushing at them with one hand, he opened the toolbox, grimacing as sticky blood from the slaughtered kangaroos smeared across his hands. He found the pinch bar and, still swatting at the flies, climbed back to the ground and levered open the passenger door of the ute.

'Is the dog hurt?' their patient asked. 'Did you take a look at him?'

'Do I look like I've got a death wish?' Nick asked, clambering into the cabin so he could examine the young man.

He laughed, although Nick sensed it was an effort, then as the slight trace of colour that had been in the young man's face drained away and his eyes closed in what looked like a faint, Nick began examining him.

'Here, gloves.'

Annabelle was at the open door, holding out a pair of gloves towards him. Nick didn't want to remind her he'd already examined the fellow at the airport without gloves and was now liberally covered with roo blood, because undoubtedly she'd meant well.

She'd also grown at least sixty centimetres taller.

'I dragged the chest down here and I'm standing on it,' she explained, setting a battery-operated blood-pressure device on the dashboard in front of him. 'So, whatever you need, just ask.'

The young man stirred as Nick pressed one hand against the patient's chest, feeling for the rise and fall that would indicate he was breathing normally.

'Hurts,' the patient managed, then he gave a gasping kind of cry.

Nick studied the man's position then the inside of the vehicle as he carefully moved his fingers across the man's ribs. A pneumothorax of some kind was likely in crash injuries, caused by damage to the ribs hitting the steering-wheel, but this vehicle had tilted and tipped rather than crashing head on, so the injury could be—

He'd found it, a small section of the bony skeleton of the chest that had obviously been torn in two places, so when the young man breathed in, this part, no longer anchored to the rest of the chest wall, didn't move with the rest, causing pain and breathing difficulty.

'He's got a flail chest. I'll need oxygen and a bag and anaesthesia. We'll also need the ambulance to take him back to town.'

Annabelle disappeared from the open door, returning what seemed like seconds later with the equipment he needed.

Nick started with the basics, slipping a mask over the young man's mouth and nose and starting oxygen flowing through it. Later, the patient might need intubation but that could wait.

Getting some local anaesthetic into the rib cage on the injured side was going to be more difficult, but they couldn't question the patient about other injuries if he kept passing out with pain. He eased the young man's body towards him and found he could reach the injured part. He swabbed the skin then pressed the needle with the local anaesthetic into an intercostal space, knowing he really needed an intercostal nerve block or epidural but not able to provide such luxuries.

But after three locals around the site, the young man's colour improved and he announced he felt much better.

Time for introductions, Nick figured.

'I'm Nick and the tall woman in the doorway is Annabelle. And you're...?'

'Steve.'

'Okay, Steve, now we've got the worst of your pain sorted, where else are you hurt?'

Steve moved cautiously, lifting one leg then the other then flexing his arms.

'I think everything else is okay,' he said gruffly. 'Hell, I thought I was dying there, it hurt so much. I couldn't move without passing out—thought a heart attack for sure.'

Nick explained about the damage to his chest and the problems with his lungs.

'But the local injections I've given you will only hold you for so long. Annabelle's called the ambulance and you'll be going back to Murrawingi for a while. The doc there will do X-rays and put you on a proper ventilator, and maybe strap those ribs to give them a chance to heal.'

'What about my roos?'

Nick shook his head.

'All too dead for me to save,' he joked, then realised the young man was seriously concerned.

'They've got to go to the chiller—it's me wages.'

'Is the chiller in Murrawingi?' Annabelle asked, no doubt understanding more of this conversation than Nick did.

'Nah! I use the one in Murrawalla. The meatworks bloke comes through that way so it makes sense to leave them closer to home.'

Chiller—meatworks—refrigeration? Nick's mind

made the connections easily enough then leapt ahead. He turned to Annabelle.

'No! No way!' he said. 'There is absolutely no way we're taking those carcasses in our vehicle.'

She looked surprised, as if she hadn't expected him to make the leap.

'We could tie them on the top,' she suggested, and Nick shook his head again.

'The man who brings the tractor can take them somewhere. He's a farmer, he must have dogs—don't they make good dog food?'

'But they're *my* roos,' Steve protested. 'And you could easily throw them up on top of the troopie and drop them at the chiller when you get to town.'

Which was how the man they called Storm set off for the town where he'd be working for the next two months with a pile of dead kangaroos on the top of his vehicle.

Fortunately the farmhand had arrived with the tractor, and not long after that the ambulance pulled up with two young, strong attendants, so he and Annabelle had little to do with the piling of the carcasses and tying them down. But the dead roos were definitely a presence as they continued their journey, making conversation both tense and terse.

'Is it okay, this killing of kangaroos?' Nick asked as Annabelle drove, easing the vehicle in and out of washouts. They were both eating the sandwiches she had bought, and Nick was learning the truth about bulldust. There was a definite crunch in the sandwich.

'It's done to cull the numbers and keep them under control. Since European civilisation brought improved pastures to land all over Australia, the kangaroo population has exploded. Back before settlement, a female kangaroo could keep a fertilised egg inside her for anything up to five years, not giving birth until she knew it would be a good season and she'd be able to feed the infant well.'

'And with improved pastures every season was a good season?' Nick asked, finding a soft drink in the cool box and opening it for her before setting it into a cup holder that had been fitted, somewhat inexpertly, to the dash.

'Not everywhere,' Annabelle admitted, 'but civilisation brought bores and pumps and dams and water troughs, and having regular water supplies also helped the population explosion. Then the farmers got angry and there was fairly wholesale slaughter, but now roo shooters are licensed and they have a specific number of roos they can shoot each season so nature is kept more or less in balance. It's because of the quota that Steve was so upset about not getting this lot to the chiller. He has to count them into his quota but wouldn't have been paid for them if he didn't bring them in so he'd have been losing some of his livelihood.'

Nick was interested enough to want to know just how much this livelihood might be—how much the carcasses on the roof of the troopie might fetch—but at that moment he caught sight of the water, running in a narrow trough not far from the edge of the road, spilling out across the land where the trough grew shallow.

'Look at the water all going to waste,' he said, and by now expected the slight smile Annabelle offered him.

'Bore water—there's an untapped bore in town, so what's not diverted into people's homes runs through channels all over the place. That's why you see the bands of green here and there—small plants growing thanks to the water.'

'But if water's so precious—and it is even in the city—why isn't it dammed or held in tanks?'

The smile broadened.

'Let's do water issues some other time,' she said, nodding her head towards the vague outlines of a cluster of buildings. 'Right now, you should be appreciating your first sight of Murrawalla.'

Nick peered ahead then, as the buildings grew closer, he counted.

'Four, five, six and maybe seven houses, if that isn't a shed attached to number six. Where do the one hundred and forty people live?'

'Most of them live on the outskirts of town,' Annabelle replied, pulling up outside what looked like a shipping container parked in a dusty corner of a roadhouse yard. 'First off, let's see if we can get someone to unload the roos.'

She slid out of the car, slapped on her new hat, and strode towards the roadhouse. Nick picked up the cast-off hat, still damp inside from its use as a basin at the airport, and tentatively fitted it on his head, then, feeling stupid, he took it off and flung it back into the cabin of the troopie. But three metres from the car he knew he needed it, returning to take it out once again and slam it firmly on his head.

Bruce gave a bark so he opened the back doors to release the dog, then heard a chorus of barks from dogs on the back of trucks and utes and lounging in the shade outside the roadhouse, and knew he'd done the wrong thing.

Again!

'Heel, boy,' he said to Bruce, and to his surprise the dog dropped obediently behind him, his damp nose close to Nick's knee. 'Good boy,' Nick told him, but his steps were very tentative as he approached the roadhouse, wondering if all the other dogs were as well trained and biddable, wondering what he'd do if he had to stop a dog fight.

Fill his hat with water and throw it over them?

Fortunately, before he had to put it to the test, Annabelle reappeared from the roadhouse, two lanky young men wearing cowboy boots and low-riding jeans trailing behind her.

'They're friends of Steve's. They'll unload the roos and sort out the payment,' Annabelle announced as the pair nodded rather shyly at Nick and kept walking.

'And now what do we do?' he asked, walking with her towards the shade of a stumpy tree. 'Shop?'

He nodded towards the roadhouse.

'We wait until they finish then go find Eileen. She's called the health manager but my guess is she's the chief cook and bottle washer at the hospital as well as the main trunk of the local grapevine. She'll fill us in with what's happening in town and what's expected of us when, and I'd say she's already got some provisions in the house for us.'

Something in the way Annabelle spoke made Nick look more closely at her, but her elfin face was giving nothing away.

'You know her, this Eileen?' he guessed, and saw a frown crease the smooth skin between Annabelle's eyebrows.

'I might do,' she said. 'I'm sure there was an Eileen

in our lives at one time, but whether it's the same one, I couldn't say.'

It was such a strange reply Nick didn't press her further, although he did notice that the frown remained, even though the question had been answered.

Annabelle watched the last roos being lifted off the troopie then headed back towards it. The flies grew thicker as she approached and she glanced at Nick to see how he was handling them.

Quite well, which was surprising. He'd picked a switch of leaves off the tree and was flapping it idly back and forth in front of his face, a good way to keep all but the most persistent ones off his face.

And with her old hat, the clothes, now even more badly scruffed, and the switch of leaves he looked, she realised, the epitome of a country man—a very good-looking country man.

You're off men and he's a womaniser, the very last type of man you want to get involved with, she reminded herself, but the fact that she'd even noticed Nick Tempest as a man was disturbing.

She kept a careful eye on him as he opened the back doors to let Bruce back in, then settled into the driver's seat. So far he'd handled this totally foreign experience really well, admitting, sometimes reluctantly, when he didn't know something and prepared to be guided by her. But Nick's reputation as a man who took control of things suggested it wouldn't be long before he adapted to the circumstances and became just as good a bush doctor as he was a city one.

Which shouldn't disturb her, but it did.

'Well?'

His demand made her turn and look at him. She'd

climbed into her seat and put on her seat belt while thinking about her companion, but her thoughts had taken her so far from the present it took her a moment to refocus.

'Hospital,' she said, and waved her hand towards the road. 'Three houses up and turn left. It's on a hill.'

Nick looked around then turned back to her and smiled.

'On a hill? There's a hill somewhere around here? I thought this country spread as flat as this all the way to Ayer's Rock.'

'There are a lot of hills, just some of them aren't very big,' Annabelle said, defending the red desert country she loved so much. 'Three houses up then turn left. You'll see a hill.'

'More an ant-heap,' Nick muttered, as he turned left and saw the low, wide-eaved building straight ahead of them. It was sheltered by the same trees he'd seen at the caravan park in Murrawingi—the ones he was fairly certain weren't willows.

He pulled up in front of the building and Annabelle jumped out, releasing Bruce from the back. The dog bounded happily up onto the veranda, where he barked once to announce he'd brought his humans safely home. Annabelle had pulled some small pink berries off the dangling branches of the tree and was rubbing them between her hands and sniffing them.

'Peppercorn trees,' she said to him, smiling as she held out her hands for him to smell the berries. 'To me, it's the smell of home.'

Nick took her hands and held them closer to his face, sniffing the distinct pepper smell while trying to ignore a sheen of tears in his companion's dark brown eyes.

He told himself they were tears of happiness—a little wash of emotion because she'd returned to a place she knew well. And he hoped he was right, because the thought of her being unhappy didn't sit well with him—not at all well. He wasn't sure why—in fact, it was downright stupid considering how capable she was—but he had begun to feel protective of this petite and soft-eyed woman, and protective wasn't an emotion he often felt around women.

# CHAPTER FOUR

EILEEN greeted them both with engulfing hugs, folding them in turn to her huge bosom but keeping her hand on Annabelle's shoulder after the hug had finished.

'So, you've come back, little Annabelle,' she said. 'Does your father know?'

'I haven't told him,' Annabelle replied, so aware of Nick's interest in the conversation she could feel it pressing against her skin.

'Someone will,' Eileen offered, then she led them into the main hall of the empty hospital, pointing out to Nick the consulting room, the two 'wards', rooms on either side of the central passageway, then the storerooms opposite a small treatment room and finally the kitchen and bathrooms right at the back.

'I've put a casserole in the fridge over at the house,' she told them, filling a kettle and setting it on the big stove. 'And I got in some basics in the way of provisions and there are biscuits in the tins so you won't starve.'

She produced a teapot, cups and saucers and was getting a cake out of a tin when she addressed Nick.

'You ever been out west before?' she asked, and Annabelle wondered how he'd answer. A lot of men she knew—men like Nick—would bluff their way through the early stages of a posting like this, but to her surprise he was honest.

'Never, and you don't need to tell me how much I don't know. Nurse Donne here has already ground my ego into the dust—bulldust, that is—and is dancing on it as we speak.'

Eileen nodded as if satisfied by his reply.

'Well, you couldn't get a better teacher than Annabelle,' she said. 'Kid brought herself up out here, and did the same for her sister. Best of the lot, those two.'

Something in the way she added the last part made Annabelle stiffen, and though she longed to ask Eileen what she meant, and a dozen other questions, she didn't want any more private revelations in front of Nick.

He was asking Eileen about their schedule, so maybe he hadn't taken any notice of the conversation, although that hope was squashed when Eileen had led them over to the small two-bedroom house and left them to get settled in.

'Your father lives out here?'

Annabelle dropped her backpack on the floor of the living room and looked at him, wondering how little she could get away with telling him.

'He's an opal miner,' she said.

'Opal miner? I thought the mine was oil?'

'Oil to the west and opals to the east, but you don't mine oil so much as drill for it. Mining camps—the big iron ore, coal or gold mines, which use fly in, fly out labour—have their own airfields and use privately contracted planes to transport their men. With oil, once the wells are drilled and capped and the pipelines built, there's very little maintenance so oil companies don't need to set up as much infrastructure, because the camp isn't permanent.'

'Neatly turning the conversation away from your father,' Nick observed, then nodded towards the two doorways leading off the living room. 'You can choose first with the bedrooms, but only on condition I get to use the bathroom first each morning because I know how long you women can take in a bathroom.'

'I'm sure you do,' Annabelle muttered to herself as she took her things through to the bedroom at the front of the house. Not that Nick's private life was any of her business, it just made her uncomfortable thinking about him and his women.

And it was probably unfair, taking the front bedroom, knowing full well the western sun would make his uncomfortably hot in the afternoons.

Too bad!

Served him right.

But as she muttered these comforting phrases to herself she did wonder why she was even thinking about him. She was there to work, and to try to sort things out between herself and her father. Nick was just the colleague she was stuck with...

Nick carted his suitcase into the other bedroom, already quite hot, although the window was open to its widest. Maybe the dust-encrusted fly screens stopped air coming in. He turned on the ceiling fan and felt cooler as the currents of air passed across his skin. He slumped down on the bed.

What in the name of fortune was he doing out here?

He rubbed his hand across his face, feeling the sweat

and the prickle of his emerging beard. It was too hot to think about it right now.

'You want first shower in the afternoon as well, or may I use the bathroom?'

He looked up to see Annabelle standing in the doorway. She was as different from the women he usually went out with as a woman could be—small, with dark hair and eyes where Nellie, and most of the women he'd taken out both before and since her, was elegantly tall and palely blonde. He stared at Annabelle for a moment, the question she'd asked forgotten as he tried to work out why he'd stuck to the type when both his fiancée and his wife had proved so un—

Un-what? Jill had probably been unfaithful but he doubted Nellie had. Nellie had been deceitful—maybe unreliable was the word that fitted both of them, though with Nellie—

Unscrupulous!

'Bathroom? Do you want first shower?'

Nick shook his head and watched her walk away with a towel slung over her shoulder and a small toiletry bag dangling from one finger.

Proximity—that was the only reason he was looking at Annabelle Donne as a woman.

Annabelle turned on the shower and grimaced at the smell.

'You'll get used to it,' she reminded herself. 'Give it a week and you won't notice it.'

But as she washed away today's layer of red dust, she was sorry she hadn't brought a perfumed soap that might have helped to mask the smell.

'Idiot!' she said, through water raining hot and hard down on her head. 'The only possible reason you would

even think such a thing is because the man you're sharing the house with is Nick Tempest. Had it been Paul,
who should have been here, would you have cared? Of
course not.'

She continued to berate herself as the water sluiced
soap from her body, though once she'd turned the water
off she had to do it silently, reminding herself Nick
Tempest was exactly the kind of man she didn't like—
the kind of man she was trying to get out of her system
by coming out here.

Once dry she spread her toiletries on a shelf above
the washbasin, careful to keep the pathetic little group—
moisturiser, shampoo, conditioner and soap—to one
side so there'd be room for Nick's things. That done,
she tucked her towel around her body and headed back
to her room, passing Nick in the sitting room, where his
eyes roved down past the towel to take in her bare legs
and back up her body, pausing where her breasts, quite
decently covered, pushed at the towel.

His eyebrows rose.

Then he sniffed the air.

'Phew! You're right about the smell!' he said, and
for some reason Annabelle felt put out. Not that she'd
expected him to make a chivalrous comment on her
legs—in fact, she'd have to remember in future to take
her clothes into the bathroom—but...

'Bathroom's free,' she said, totally unnecessarily, and
continued on into her room, shutting the door behind
her but not able to shut out the way he'd looked at her.

Looked at her and found her wanting, though most
women would pale into insignificance compared to
that model Nellie who'd been his wife. The worrying

thing was that it had disturbed her—the look *and* lack of comment—in a way she didn't want to think about.

She dressed quickly and set off across the yard to the hospital, patting Bruce who'd nosed up to her legs as soon as she'd stepped outside.

Eileen was sitting at the kitchen table, no doubt waiting for her.

'He's a handsome one you've got there,' Eileen greeted her, waving a hand towards a chair. 'But he has that glint in his eye like your father has. I thought you'd have been too smart to fall for that type.'

'He's not mine and I haven't fallen for him. He's a fill-in doctor and I'm a fill-in nurse.' She paused, then asked the question she should have asked earlier. 'How's Dad?'

Eileen nodded.

'He's good. Healthwise strong as a horse—on a good seam, he says. Betsy-Ann's out there at the moment.'

Which explained Eileen's earlier comment, Betsy-Ann being one of the sisters Annabelle had not been responsible for bringing up—Betsy-Ann and Molly-May, the boats as Annabelle and Kitty had always called them, sure their names were more suitable to dinghies than real-life women. But if her father was finding good opal in the mine, then one or other of the sisters *would* be there, determined to get what they could out of him.

'Anyone else?' Annabelle asked, knowing Eileen would understand the question.

'Not for over a year,' she said. 'There was a young German tourist got mixed up with him and stayed out there for a while, but there's been no one permanent—or as permanent as your father gets—for, oh, probably six or seven years.'

So it wasn't because of a woman he hadn't answered her plea for help, Annabelle thought, but she didn't say it because Eileen had always been good to her and, worse, had loved her father.

'He's always wasted love,' Annabelle said instead. 'Not treasured it the way it should be treasured.'

Eileen nodded, then, as most women who'd been involved with Gerald Donne did, she excused him.

'It's the fever, love,' she said, patting Annabelle's hand. 'He can't help it—it's not as if you can take an antibiotic and opal fever will go away. The opal comes first, second, third and probably way down to fifty-seventh with him. The rest of us, we've just had to fit in where we can and take whatever he's prepared to offer us.'

'That's hardly fair, is it?' Annabelle muttered, already wondering if coming out here would achieve anything other than more heartache.

'Is that why you've come?' Eileen asked. 'To tell him what's fair and what isn't?'

'As if he'd take any notice,' Annabelle replied. 'No, I came to make peace with him.'

It sounded a little too pat, possibly because it was. The reason she'd come was far deeper and more complex than that, but how to explain to one of her father's ex-lovers that she'd come so she could meet him as an adult and to find out why he'd deserted her and Kitty. Perhaps then she'd be able to understand why Graham had deceived her so easily—to understand and, finally, to accept…

\* \* \*

She'd missed the sunsets.

The thought struck her with such force as she made her way back to the house behind the hospital that she stopped and gazed up at the sky, the tall eucalypt behind the house black against the scarlet, and vermillion, and orange, and rich pink of the evening sky.

The colours of the best opal…

'I'm cooking dinner.'

Nick's greeting as she came through the door brought her out of the past, and she frowned for a moment, trying to make sense of what he was saying, eventually laughing when she saw the casserole dish in his hands.

'Well, I've taken it out of the refrigerator, but I'm not entirely sure if it's a microwave deal or if we need the oven on. Seems to me we could put it in my bedroom if it needs an oven.'

'Definitely microwave. We'll keep the oven for roast lamb on a cold blustery night.'

Something shifted in the atmosphere of the room, as if a wind had sighed between them. Had Nick felt it, too, that he was frowning at her?

Not that he said anything, merely muttering about the chance of a cold blustery night in hell being just as likely, while settling the casserole dish in the microwave, frowning again for a few seconds as he sorted out the dials then starting it heating.

Of course, nothing had shifted in the atmosphere between them, Annabelle told herself. What atmosphere anyway?

But she'd been right. Nick's question as they sat at the dinner table proved it.

'Do you find the false intimacy of this arrangement uncomfortable?'

Annabelle, who'd been concentrating very hard on not spilling peas off her fork in order to ignore the discomfort she felt sitting opposite Nick at the table, glanced up at him.

'False intimacy?' she repeated, although he'd put his finger right on it—encapsulating in two words her physical and mental discomfort.

Not that she'd admit it!

Not in a thousand years…

'Haven't you ever shared a house with someone before?' she asked, fending off a reply.

Blue eyes she'd been desperately trying to avoid met hers across the table.

'Only with my parents and then my wife—ex-wife, I suppose I should say.'

As a conversation stopper it was unbeatable, but surely talking was preferable to trying to pretend he wasn't there.

'The model?'

Well, everyone knew about it so why not say it out loud?

'The model!' he confirmed, anger flaring in the blue eyes. But it was the pain intermingled with it that made Annabelle regret her impulse to tease him.

'I'm sorry!' She blurted out the words, although the platitude would never be enough. 'That was rude of me. To you she'd have been a person first—the modelling just a job—and actually, yes, I do find our situation uncomfortable, but I think that's natural enough as we don't know each other all that well. Mind you,' she rushed on, hoping to get over the shame she felt at her insensitive remark, 'I've lived in shared houses—you know, renting a room in a house—with strangers but I always had Kitty, my sister, with me, so that was different.'

Nick regarded the woman across the table, pink with what he suspected was mortification, rushing into words to cover her confusion, although the remark had been little more than a natural response for all it had struck home with him because it had been the model, not the person who'd made the decision—if that made sense.

But back in the present, why would Annabelle be so sensitive to hurt in other people?

Because she'd been hurt herself?

Two months—they'd hardly get to know each other well enough for him to find out, which, for some reason, caused a twinge of regret.

She was back to balancing peas on her fork and he sought some neutral kind of conversation to break what was becoming an uncomfortable silence.

'So, this sister Kitty, is she the one studying medicine?'

The dark eyes lifted from her plate but before she could reply the phone rang. Annabelle was first to her feet, leaping up as if escaping from something worse than a little awkwardness.

Nick listened but her side of the conversation was hardly illuminating.

'You did the right thing with the clean, wet cloth. Radio the car to say we'll be waiting at the hospital.'

'Problem?' he asked as she slid back into her seat.

'Yes, but far enough away for us to finish dinner first. One of the riggers has caught his hand in some moving part of their machinery. The first-aid bloke out there says lacerated skin and query torn tendons but he thinks no broken bones. Someone's driving the patient in, ETA here in thirty minutes.'

'We'll X-ray it anyway. Good thing we checked out the machine when Eileen was showing us the hospital,' Nick said, then he chuckled. 'Good grief, I sound like one of the doctors on a television show, saying everything out loud so the audience knows what's going on.'

Annabelle grinned at him and he felt relief sweep through him, making him wonder if the awkwardness of their earlier conversation had disturbed him more than he'd realised.

The laceration was severe and Nick knew if the man had come into the ER, the staff would have called in a hand specialist, but the ER was fifteen hundred kilometres away so it was up to him and Annabelle to do the best they could.

'How did it happen?' he asked their patient, now introduced as Max, while Annabelle finished unwrapping the loose dressing from the hand.

'Caught it in the pipe joiner,' Max told him, and Nick glanced quickly at Annabelle to see if 'pipe joiner' meant any more to her than it did to him.

Did Max catch the glance and the slight shrug of Annabelle's shoulders that he followed up with more explanation?

'We have to keep feeding more pipes into the hole we're drilling so we can bring up core samples from deeper levels.'

He might still have been talking a foreign language, but Nick nodded as if it all made perfect sense. What didn't make sense was the wound, because skin was torn back off the upper surface of the hand while a deep cut on the palmar surface of the right forefinger suggested the possibility of tendon damage. He tried to imagine a situation where both sides of the hand would be involved and shuddered at his thoughts.

Annabelle was flushing saline into the open wounds with a 60cc syringe and a wide-gauge needle, squirting fluid deep under the torn skin to clean out any foreign matter.

'I need to poke around a bit in the finger wound,' Nick said to Max, 'so I'll shoot some local anaesthetic in. You're right handed?'

'Totally hopeless with my left so I hope you can put this back together,' Max told him, while Annabelle stopped flushing the wounds long enough to hand Nick the anaesthetic he would need.

'So if there's tendon damage, you'll need to repair it?' she murmured to Nick, as Max gave them chapter and verse on his uselessness with his left hand.

'*We'll* have to repair it,' Nick murmured back. 'Can you check out what we have in fine sutures? Six would be great. I'll X-ray it in case there are broken or crushed bones.'

'The bloke at the camp—our first-aid guy—said the bones were okay,' Max told Nick, as he took the angled shots he needed to actually prove the 'first-aid guy' right.

'Best to be sure,' he said, knowing how easy it was to miss a displaced or damaged metacarpal or phalange.

But having made sure, he had to get down to business.

'We'll close the tears on the back of the hand with tissue adhesives rather than sutures,' Nick said. 'Research shows the wounds heal just as well, if not better. It'll be much faster than suturing, and once done we can turn your hand over and look at the nasty mess on the other side that much sooner.'

'I'll do this bit,' Annabelle added. 'I love doing jigsaws.'

Nick watched as her nimble fingers eased the torn skin into place, holding the edges together so he could apply a tiny strip of silk tape to keep it there. She *was* good, he realised, tutting away to herself when she couldn't get the edges of the wound properly aligned, her face a study in concentration.

The job necessitated them standing close together, and although a lot of work in the ER meant working in close proximity—that word again—with a colleague, this was somehow different.

'Ready!'

Annabelle's voice brought him out of his uncomfortable thoughts and he slid another adhesive strip over the wound she'd closed and concentrated on the task at hand.

'It does look like a jigsaw,' Max declared, when they'd finished and Nick was applying an antibiotic ointment before Annabelle fitted a dressing over the lot.

'The dressing stays for forty-eight hours and the strips will slough off in about a week—at the most ten days,' Nick told their patient. 'But as your hand will be bound up anyway, you shouldn't have a problem with the strips.'

He turned his attention to the torn skin and deep gash on the inner side of Max's forefinger. A proper tendon repair would require wire or needles through the tendon on either side of the repair site to prevent contraction but that was a job for a specialist. Nick probed the wound and found, to his relief, the tendon torn, but only partially.

Partial tendon repairs were a different thing altogether. Not only were partial tendon repairs regularly carried out in the ER, but he'd had some experience of them himself. He knew they could be sutured but that often led to complications with adhesions, whereas if he could trim the lacerated tendon without leaving it too weak to function, Max should have full movement in his finger once the wound had healed.

Annabelle was flushing the wound so he could see the tendon but not clearly enough.

Did she guess this that she handed him a loupe?

'Ah,' he said, pointing to the thread-like strip that had torn loose, 'see it there?'

She was pressed close to his side now, her shiny cap of hair just below his chin, but this time instead of awkwardness he felt the bond of colleagues, working together to achieve the best possible outcome for their patient.

The positivity of the thought lifted his spirits and he carefully trimmed the tendon then cut away torn skin and sutured the wound above it, applying antibiotic ointment once again, before asking Annabelle for a splint to hold the finger immobile while the wounds healed.

'I can get back to work, then?' Max asked, as Annabelle finished wrapping his hand.

'No way!' Nick's reply was prompt and firm. 'You've just told us you're useless with your left hand. That finger in particular has to heal. You can take the dressing off the back of your hand and leave it open in a couple of days, but you saw it for yourself. You get back to work and get an infection in one of those tears and you'll be off for a lot longer than a week or two.'

'A week or two? What am I expected to do out there for a week or two?'

'Office work? Filing?' Annabelle offered helpfully, earning a look of loathing from Max.

'That's just what the boss'll say,' he muttered. 'I should have done a proper job on it and been sent to Brisbane.'

'Where your wife could fuss over you?' Nick asked, having seen the wedding ring on the man's hand.

'That'd be less likely than the boss at the camp telling me to take time off,' Max told him. 'My wife's a worker—nine to five and all the overtime she can get. What she'd want is for me to have the dinner cooked when she gets home and the shopping done, not to mention the washing.'

Nick wanted to laugh but Max sounded seriously put out over this state of affairs. Annabelle obviously had no such qualms. She chuckled, a deep, rich, happy sound.

'Poor Max,' she said, sarcasm dripping from the words, 'having to choose between filing and housework!'

'Well, it's not as if I don't help out at home,' Max protested. 'When I'm there, that is, but what I say is that if I'm earning big money like I am at the rig, then surely when I'm home she should be there with me.'

'Except that jobs don't work that way,' Annabelle reminded him. 'I bet you're both working for a reason.'

He nodded and looked somewhat embarrassed.

'Yeah,' he admitted grudgingly, 'we want to buy a house but we don't want to be lumbered with a huge mortgage, so if we both work really hard for five years, we'll be able to put down a decent deposit.'

'And how many years have you got to go?' Nick felt it was time he entered the conversation again, although he'd enjoyed the way Annabelle had got Max talking, the conversation soothing his agitation over the injury.

'Two!' Max declared. 'And we know just where we want to build. When we're both at home at the same time, we go for drives and look at land and—'

'Am I taking you back to camp?'

Max's description of his home-to-be was interrupted by the arrival of the man who'd driven him to town, and who had, no doubt, been enjoying a snack, if not a drink, at the pub while he waited.

'Yeah!' Max told him, sounding far more accepting of his fate than he had earlier. 'Thanks, Doc, thanks, Nurse. See you soon.'

'Hold on, we're not quite done,' Nick told him, as Annabelle appeared from the dispensary with a bottle of antibiotics. Nick checked the label and saw she'd already typed out the instructions, thinking ahead all the time.

'Three times a day,' he told Max, handing him the bottle. 'We've a clinic at the camp during the week, so we'll check on your hand then, but if you see any redness or feel tenderness and pain around the skin wounds, let us know.'

Nick walked the pair to the front door, returning to the small outpatient room to find Annabelle had tidied everything away. In fact, it looked as clean and neat as it had before their patient had arrived.

Very much as it had looked then, for not even the nurse was present. He peered into the equipment cupboard and checked the X-ray room but there was no sign of Annabelle.

Feeling put out that she'd obviously gone home

without waiting for him, he made his way out through the empty building and across the small yard to the house they shared.

It too, was empty, her wide-open bedroom door revealing the entire room so unless she was hiding under the bed, she hadn't returned to the house. He was telling himself it was none of his business where she was when he heard the scrunch of shoes on the hard-baked earth and looked out through the open back door to see her standing at the top of their 'hill', silhouetted against the night sky.

Drawn by something beautiful in that solitary figure, he walked towards her, coming to stand beside her, looking west across an apparently endless moonlit plain, looking up to a sky that stretched for ever.

Had she sensed his arrival that she spoke almost as soon as he came to a halt beside her, close but not too close?

'Once I had a man like that. We'd go for drives from time to time and look at land and talk of houses we would build, of the family we would have.'

The deadness in her usually vibrant voice told him this was not a happy-ending story and the urge to put a comforting arm around her was so strong he had to shuffle a little sideways to make the movement impossible.

'Trouble was it turned out he already had a family and a house, complete with wife and two children.'

She shuddered, or maybe shook herself, shaking off the memories, and turned to him with a smile that even by moonlight he could tell was wan.

'Sorry! I didn't think it could get to me any more, but at least out here a person can get things into perspective again.'

She stretched her arms wide, encompassing land that stretched for ever until it disappeared into the darkness of the night.

'How can you look out there and not realise how insignificant your problems are? They call the Outback big-sky country, you can see why, can't you?'

She spoke quietly, but to Nick's relief her voice was strong again. Earlier the pain in it had stabbed into his heart, although how a man still battling to come to terms with his own pain could take on someone else's he had no idea, for all his immediate urge had been to give her a hug.

Now, looking around, Nick had to agree, both with her comment about the insignificance of personal problems and with the broad sweep of the sky. Never before had he appreciated the enormity of the heavens above him and the sheer number and brightness of the stars, planets and constellations.

'Beautiful,' he murmured, then looked down at the face of the woman beside him. Lit by the radiance of stars and moon, lit, now, from within by some special connection she obviously had with this country, the same word definitely applied to her.

'Beautiful,' he repeated, and only an iron will stopped him from sealing the word by dropping a kiss on those quirky, tantalising lips.

A comforting kiss, that was all it would have been, like the hug, he told himself as he followed her back to the house.

# CHAPTER FIVE

THE intimacy thing—Annabelle had adopted Nick's description of the awkwardness between them—was absent next morning, both of them sleeping late and inevitably having to rush. They passed each other in the kitchen as Nick came in, gleaming clean and utterly gorgeous in his country gear, ready to get his breakfast, and Annabelle, having breakfasted but still in the tattered T-shirt that did service as a nightgown, scuttled to the bathroom.

Memories of her pathetic moonlight confession returned as she stood under the water, and she cringed, wondering how on earth she could face the man again. But face him she had to, so it was best to pretend it had never happened and hope and pray he wouldn't mention it.

Talk about stupid!

She was over Graham, right over him, yet Max's words about the bit of land had—

Forget it!

She scrubbed the towel across her body, glad it was a rough hospital issue one and the brisk rub scratched enough to bring her back to her senses.

Now all she had to do was face the man who knew her shame.

'Big day, yesterday.'

Nick stating the obvious as they crossed to the hospital for their first clinic session told Annabelle the awkwardness between them wasn't completely gone, but also reassured her that he was unlikely to mention the personal part of the evening.

As for the awkwardness, it was unlikely it would ever go as far as she was concerned, for there was something about Nick that disturbed her in ways she didn't understand. It wasn't physical attraction—at least not entirely. A thousand-year-old Egyptian mummy would probably find Nick physically attractive. No, it was something more, something deeper, some suspicion that there was more to him than the popular image he seemed so determined to present.

Trailing behind him as they entered the hospital, she shook her head, hoping to rid it of the distracting thoughts. Work awaited her—awaited them both—and knowing country folk she was reasonably certain most of the town would turn up for an appointment, just to get a look at the new medical team.

This prophecy was confirmed as she walked onto the front veranda, which served as a waiting room.

'Ha, Annabelle Donne, someone said you'd become a nurse. And now you're back where you belong, you gonna stay?'

Old Mrs Fairchild, once a nurse at this hospital herself, was the first to recognise Annabelle.

'Only for two months,' Annabelle replied. 'Now, who's first here?'

Three people leapt to their feet but before trouble could erupt Eileen appeared.

'You go into the consulting room with the doc,' she ordered Annabelle. 'I've got all the records out and I'll send them through in order, otherwise it will be a rabble.'

She waved a piece of paper in the air and Annabelle realised she had a list. Knowing Eileen, she'd have sorted them in order of urgency, not arrival time, which would cause some chaos on the veranda, but if anyone could handle it, Eileen could.

'Jane Crenshaw, twenty-nine weeks pregnant, in for a regular check-up but the note from Eileen has a question mark after "regular". Seems she was in last week as well and her check-ups have been fortnightly.'

Nick was frowning slightly as he perused the notes, probably wondering about the change in routine.

'The Crenshaws have a big property about fifty kilometres north so she wouldn't have driven in just to check out the new staff,' Annabelle told him. 'Maybe she's moved onto weekly visits.'

'That would be unusual before the last month of pregnancy unless there was a problem, but I suspect the best thing to do is to stop guessing and see her.' Nick grinned as he made this declaration and Annabelle realised he'd been a little apprehensive about this first appointment in this, to him, foreign land.

In the ER, even in the most hectic and tumultuous situations, he was cool and competent—more than competent, really, an excellent doctor. But as a man who prided himself on his professional expertise, perhaps it was only natural he'd be a little wary about what lay ahead in such a different situation.

Annabelle went to the door to call Jane in, smiling as she realised the woman had been Jane Wilson. As children they'd competed against each other at School of the Air sports days and eisteddfods.

'Annabelle!' Jane's large baby bump made hugging awkward, but the hug gave Annabelle a close-up look at the greyness of Jane's skin and the shadows under her eyes.

Holding Jane's arm to steady her—the woman looked as if she might pass out at any moment—Annabelle led her to the examination couch and helped her sit on it, before introducing her to Nick.

'Annabelle will weigh you and take a urine sample when we finish,' he said gently, 'but tell me, is something bothering you that you came in today?'

Jane shook her head, but her eyes were brimming with tears that threatened to overflow until, by some effort of will, she stopped them, blinked, sniffed, then offered Nick a wan smile.

'This is going to sound stupid, because there's nothing wrong—nothing different that I can pinpoint, although because it's my first baby I don't know how things should be, but I'm worried. Something doesn't feel right—not physically like pain or discomfort, although a bit of discomfort's always there, but some feeling inside me that things aren't right.'

In the ER, although the medical staff might be the first to see a pregnant woman, any problems were soon passed on to the obstetrician on call, but six months of an obstetrics placement during his intern years meant training took over as Nick began to examine his patient.

The mother first—pulse, blood pressure, general well-being.

'You're eating well? No nausea? What about cramps?'

'Only in my calves, although some friends I talk to on the internet are having quite severe cramps—they've got some name...'

'Braxton-Hicks' contractions,' Nick told her, as he examined her ankles for oedema. 'False labour and quite common in the third trimester of your pregnancy, but you haven't been having those?'

Jane shook her head.

'Like I said,' she told him, a catch in her voice, 'there's really nothing wrong with me.'

But there was. Nick knew that it was possible for a patient to be aware of a problem before it could be diagnosed and from the frown on Annabelle's face, she also knew it.

'Well, let's examine the kid now,' he said, smiling at Jane and winning a small smile in response.

Measurement of the fundal height confirmed foetal growth was normal, and the simple counting of the foetal heartbeats through a stethoscope confirmed the baby's heart was strong and healthy.

'Are you still feeling movement?' Nick asked, but even as he spoke he saw what could only be a small foot distending the skin on its mother's abdomen.

'All the time,' Jane replied. 'If that'd stopped, I'd have reason to be worried.'

Anxiety had returned to her voice and her face was drawn.

'How are you sleeping?' Nick asked her and she sighed.

'Well, it's hard because it's not particularly comfortable and then when I wake up I worry, and it takes ages to get back to sleep. Col, my husband, he's great, but he's mustering at the moment so he's not there to rub my back or tell me I'm being silly.'

Now the tears did spill over and Nick wondered if it was her husband's absence that lay at the core of her concern. For a moment he hesitated, then thought, to hell with showing ignorance, and he asked, 'How long is he away for?'

Jane found a small smile.

'It should only be a few more days, and a few weeks after he gets back he's driving me to Brisbane. We decided right at the beginning we'd have the baby there and I've a specialist booked. I saw him early on when we were down for the show, and whatever doctor has been here sends my details down to him.'

Nick checked the notes and saw the name of a specialist he knew.

'Look,' he said to Jane, 'I've a line-up of patients out there so I can't do it now, but I'll phone your specialist later and have a chat to him and get him to phone you if he has any questions.'

He hesitated, annoyed that he didn't know more of how things worked in the country, then added, 'If your husband's away, why not stay in town for a few days? You don't have to stay at the hospital, although we'd be happy to have you here, but you could stay at the motel or the pub, and that way you're close by if you notice any changes.'

Jane smiled—a better smile this time.

'And who'd feed the dogs and the horses? Most of the dogs are gone, of course, and some of the horses, but the old dogs don't go out on the big muster any more. Then there's the generator to be turned on while the pump's going to fill the yard tank and the garden to be watered, and if I don't get on to making lemon butter soon, the place will be overrun by lemons. Actually...' she stood up and delved into the large handbag she'd left on a chair '...I brought some lemons in for you, thinking Eileen could use them, but I guess Annabelle will remember how to make lemon butter.'

'I'm still back with you feeding dogs and horses. What happens when you go to Brisbane to have the baby? Will your husband stay home?'

'Oh, no, he wouldn't miss the birth for the world. We'll get farm sitters in, they're already booked, and in an emergency the neighbours are always good, although they live forty k away.'

She made it sound so ordinary, this life she led, Nick could only shake his head. He said goodbye and as Annabelle led Jane away to the small treatment room, he opened the door to the veranda and called in the next patient.

To Annabelle the day flew by, greeting old acquaintances and meeting new arrivals to the town. Knowing Nick's reputation in the ER, she wasn't surprised at his efficiency, but his kindness to each and every patient— his patience, in fact—won her admiration. He treated every person as if he had all the time in the world, in spite of the fact half the town had gathered on the veranda.

He even felt for a lump in the neck of Mrs Warren's old dog, Oscar, finding the fibrous swelling and assuring the elderly woman that it wasn't serious.

'I'll check it out on the internet this evening,' he told her as she departed, clutching her heart pills, although Annabelle was certain it was Oscar's health that had brought her to the hospital. 'If it's anything serious, I'll get in touch.'

Yet throughout the day Annabelle was aware that Nick had changed in some way, as if, for all his smiles and kindnesses, he'd closed off some part of himself.

As if you know him well enough to make that kind of judgement, she chided herself, but the feeling persisted, especially as, the moment they returned to their little house, he settled on the couch with his laptop open on his knee, cutting himself off from any conversation.

Not that Annabelle needed conversation. Their last-but-one patient, Bill Green, from Yarrawonga station, had brought in what seemed like half a beast, presenting it to Annabelle in two cool boxes, with a laconic 'We killed a couple of days ago and thought you could use some decent meat.'

While Nick had been phoning the obstetrician in Brisbane, Annabelle had lugged the cool boxes home and was now in the kitchen, battling to sort the meat into meal-sized portions so she could freeze it for future use.

She muttered an oath to herself as a T-bone steak the size of New South Wales fell to the kitchen floor.

Was Nick not used to women swearing that she finally got his attention?

'What *are* you doing?' he demanded, not moving from the couch but at least looking towards her.

'Wrestling bits of meat into submission. One of our patients has kindly donated most of a bullock for our culinary enjoyment, but as it's unlikely we could eat even a hundredth of it in one go, I'm packing it and freezing it.'

'A bullock?'

*Now* he was on his feet, crossing the living area in two strides and peering over the breakfast bar to the island bench, where she was trying to sort the meat into some kind of order.

'You know, I've never seen meat in the wild so to speak. I know Mum always had a butcher, but my meat comes on little trays all wrapped and labelled at the supermarket—usually with instructions on how to cook it. How do you know which bit is which and what it's meant for?'

Annbelle thought about lying then shrugged and admitted, 'It's mainly guesswork so far. I mean, I know these are T-bones...' she held one up '...and that long bit there is rib fillet and the smaller long bit probably eye fillet, but these huge lumps, well, they could be rump or round or whatever else beef comes in. Financial constraints in my life mean I mainly eat vegetables and sausages, but obviously the sausages come ready made.'

Nick chuckled and she felt a wash of warmth through her body. Maybe she'd imagined his distraction.

'Can I help?' he offered.

She smiled at him, eyebrows raised, and he lifted his arms in surrender.

'Okay, stupid offer. I wouldn't have a clue but if you think we should chop up some of those big bits into stewing kind of steak, I could do that.'

And stand right beside her at the bench? Distracted or not, the man's presence was having an unwelcome effect on Annabelle's body and she'd already figured the only way to counter it was to keep her distance. Fortunately, before she could think of a polite way to refuse his offer, they heard Eileen announcing her presence at the door.

'Heard Bill had brought you in some beef,' she said, as she came in. 'I'll deal with it, although there's already half a bullock in the hospital freezer that he brought in for the last lot out here. He seems to think city folk don't get enough meat in their diet. What we might have to do is put on a big barbeque one night at the hospital— maybe a fundraiser for the flying doctor—and get rid of a lot of it.'

She bustled into the kitchen, shooing Annabelle out of the way, packing all but two pieces of the meat back into the ice boxes and ordering Nick to carry them over to the hospital.

'Those two steaks will do for your dinner,' she said to Annabelle. 'There's a little gas barbeque out the back you can use. It's still warm enough to eat out there. And there are plenty of ingredients for a salad in the fridge, and potatoes under the sink. I guess Nick likes a spud with his dinner.'

Nick lingered at the hospital, chatting to Eileen for a while before phoning a vet friend to ask about Oscar the dog's fibroma, so he returned to the mouthwatering smell of onions on a barbeque. He followed his nose to the small back patio, where Annabelle had dusted down the cane furniture, spread a cloth on the small table and was standing over the onions, moving them around so they would caramelise rather than burn.

'Good, you're back,' she greeted him. 'I didn't want to put the steaks on until you arrived in case you like yours rare. I like mine fairly rare—not still mooing, mind you—but if you're a burnt-to-a-crisp man, I can do that as well.'

Nick studied her for a moment, wondering if it was because they were out of the confines of the house that he was no longer feeling the awkward intimacy he'd experienced the previous day.

Or had the experience of that long day shaken it all out of him, so he could go forward in confidence with this new colleague?

A new colleague who apparently nursed a hurt as deep as his, though why he'd think of that right now he had no idea.

'Rare? Crispy?'

The questions puzzled him until he realised she'd asked a question earlier and his distraction with the change in atmosphere and memories of her moonlight confession meant he hadn't replied.

'Medium rare—definitely not mooing,' he told her, 'but isn't the barbeque a man's domain?'

He moved towards her but she waved her barbeque fork at him.

'This from a man who cooked a casserole last night?' she teased. 'You sit down and enjoy the end of the sunset. There are a couple of cans of light beer in the cool box beside the chair. I've already opened mine as the onions needed a bit of it.'

Nick stared at her for a moment longer, realising that it was the naturalness of her behaviour—her acceptance that the two of them were colleagues thrust together— that was making it easier for him to fit in. He sat as ordered and opened a beer, relaxing for the first time that day. Jane Crenshaw's arrival as their first patient had awoken his own hidden pain—pain he kept telling himself he no longer felt—so he'd had to battle to keep his composure in front of all the other patients.

Now he looked out past another of the pepper-corn trees to a sky that had darkened to purple with a thin stripe of still vivid pink marking the horizon. He breathed in the clean air, heavily scented now with searing meat and onions, and felt a wave of well-being pass over his body, relaxing tense muscles and even freeing his mind from memories.

A steak and a beer, a pretty woman turning onions— what more could a man ask for? He smiled to himself, sure it was politically incorrect to be so happy with the situation, but he *had* cooked dinner the previous night, so it was Annabelle's turn. He closed his eyes and re-laxed against the back of the chair, then opened them to find the cook had disappeared.

'I did the potatoes in the microwave—would you like yours singed a bit on the barbie?' she asked, returning with a tray that held plates, salt and pepper grinders and an assortment of bottled sauces. 'Apparently everyone who stays here has their own taste in sauce so we've plenty to choose from.'

She set the tray on the table, and when he agreed he'd like his potato singed a little on the barbeque, she used tongs to lift it and turn it, finally serving up a meal that smelled so good he fell on it with gusto.

'This meat is unbelievable,' he said, finally stop-ping for long enough to speak. 'Do we have more the same?'

Annabelle chuckled.

'So much more you'll be pleading for a nice bit of lamb before we're through, although a lot of the proper-ties out this way still have sheep so half a sheep could arrive any day.'

'For our nice roast lamb on a cold and blustery night.'

The words she'd spoken the previous evening were

out before Nick considered them, but they conjured up such an image of cosiness, he could see the pair of them huddled together in a blanket in front of the little wood-burning stove in the living room.

The feel of Annabelle's small curvy body against his was so real, he felt his libido stirring, and quickly blanked out the image with a dampening 'Not that I can imagine this place ever being cold and blustery!'

It can be very cold and blustery, especially when the westerly winds blow, Annabelle wanted to tell him, but his words had raised the weirdest image in her mind—an image of her and Nick huddled together in a blanket in front of the fire while the smell of roasting lamb permeated the house.

It was so homely it was dangerous, and she'd have to sort out whatever part of her brain was throwing up such ridiculous ideas.

And soon!

Two days into the placement, and she was having hallucinations of togetherness, the very last thing she wanted in her life—particularly with someone like Nick Tempest.

She stood up and called to Bruce, giving him the bones from the T-bone to gnaw on—togetherness with a dog was okay!

They'd settled the previous evening on the arrangement of whoever cooked didn't have to do the dishes, so once again, when the phone rang shortly after they'd come indoors after dinner, it was Annabelle who answered it.

'We'll be right there. Turn left five k past the jump-up. Call the flying doctors then lie down with your feet up,' Nick heard her say, and wondered what on earth a

jump-up might be as he washed the detergent off his
hands and dried them.

'Jane Crenshaw,' Annabelle said. 'Her waters have
broken. I've told her—'

'I heard. Let's see what the hospital can provide in
the way of obstetric and neonatal drugs. Did you say she
lived fifty k out of town this morning? How long do the
flying doctors take?'

'That depends on whether they've a plane in
Longreach or if someone will have to fly in from Mount
Isa. Either way, by the time they rally crew and get air-
borne we'll be there first, which is just as well as we'll
have to check the airstrip for cattle and make sure the
lights work.'

As well as delivering a ten-week-premmie baby, Nick
thought, but they were at the hospital by now and he was
searching for drugs they might need. If her waters had
broken, should they try to stop labour advancing with a
drug like magnesium sulphate? He'd take some just in
case. Then there was the baby—steroids for its lungs.
Betamethasone—yes!

The triumph he felt at finding the drug was probably
out of all proportion to the problem, but if this baby was
on the way, he was going to do everything he could to
make sure it arrived safely and had the very best chance
of a healthy life.

'You drive and I'll phone the obstetrician,' he said to
Annabelle as they hurried to the troopie.

She glanced his way and he guessed she'd already
decided she'd do the driving, but she said nothing until,
remembering her phone conversation, he had to ask.

'What's a jump-up?'

She turned to him and grinned.

'You'll understand when you see it, but it's really nothing more than a hill, or maybe a ridge, that rises out of the ground, then drops away again.'

Jump-up! Nick added the word to his new vocabulary, along with troopie and bulldust and roo chiller, so he was smiling as he pressed the obstetrician's number into his mobile.

'He says if labour's already advanced and dilatation present, not to try to stop it. Will the flying doctors bring someone with premmie experience and a special crib?'

'Definitely!' Annabelle assured him. 'They're set up for this kind of thing and either the doctor or the nurse will know neonatal procedures. That's one reason it might take them longer to get there, finding the right people and organising gear, but they won't be far behind us. And now you're off the phone, I'll speed up and you can watch for roos or other animals.'

'Other animals?'

'Cattle, wild pigs, camels—we're too far south for buffaloes.'

'Camels? Buffaloes?'

She was having him on, he was sure, but still the disbelieving words escaped his lips.

'Both were introduced in the early years of settlement, camels to cross the central desert when they laid the telegraph wires up the centre, and buffaloes—well, I'm not sure why they came, but they loved the place once they got here and bred like mad, but, as I said, they're further north and stay around the wetlands.'

A quiver of disquiet that he knew so little about his country led to a determination to learn more—wherever and whenever he could. And for this area, what better teacher could he have than Annabelle? He was about to ask her about the wild pigs when he saw the shadows leaping across the road ahead.

'Roos!' he said, and she braked and slowed, but the animals had bounded off the road before they reached them.

He forgot about learning more about the country and concentrated on keeping watch, warning her in time to slow when he noticed a group of cattle camped on the road.

'It's warm from the sun,' his guide explained, as she edged her way through the reluctant-to-move beasts.

Then they were driving uphill and he recognised her description of the jump-up, rising without warning, cresting for perhaps twenty yards then dropping back again.

A quarter of an hour later they stopped at the bottom of the steps of a new-looking farmhouse, wide and low, with an overreaching roof shading a wide veranda.

'Jane, we're here. Call out so we can find you.'

Annabelle entered the house first, calling to their patient, who replied from somewhere to the right.

They found Jane in the bedroom, obediently lying flat with her feet propped on a pile of pillows. She was pale, and faint tearstains clung to her cheeks, but the look of determination on her face told Nick she'd handle whatever lay ahead of her.

'I radioed Col, he's coming home. I just hope he makes it before the flying doctor.'

And I hope he doesn't drive like a madman and kill himself on the way, Annabelle thought, knowing how some country men raced along the Outback tracks. Nick was already examining Jane, talking to her all the time, telling her he'd spoken to the obstetrician and assuring her that even if the baby came, thirty weeks wasn't too early these days.

'It's definitely coming,' Jane told him, and Annabelle knew she was right as she watched a contraction move Jane's belly.

'So, we'll give him something for his lungs, and give you some fluid so you don't dehydrate,' Nick said, preparing an injection while Annabelle wondered if all men automatically assumed babies would be boys.

Although, she admitted to herself, it was better calling the baby him rather than it.

But him or her, the baby would need to be kept warm and wrapped in something soft.

'Where's your linen cupboard?' she asked, and when Jane explained Annabelle headed there, finding towels first to put under Jane for the birth, then rummaging around, smiling when she discovered a hot-water bottle. The kitchen was easy to find and as the kettle boiled she checked out the pantry, finally emptying a collection of glass jars out of a cardboard box.

Covered in a folded sheet, with the hot-water bottle wrapped in a towel set in the bottom of it, the box would make a perfect little bassinette for Baby Crenshaw.

Another search of the linen cupboard produced a medical chest and in it a fine muslin sling, which would do to protect the baby's skin.

Annabelle returned to the bedroom with her treasures, and set them down. Jane had an oxygen mask in her hand and was breathing from it intermittently, talking to Nick all the time between groans of pain as contractions seized her.

With a video of what could lie ahead running through

her mind, Annabelle cleared the dressing table, found a cloth and wiped it down, then went back to the linen cupboard for more towels. A search through cupboards in spare bedrooms revealed a small fan heater and she returned to the bedroom and plugged this in, turning it on but directed towards the dressing table, before spreading out the towels. The table should be heated and she solved that problem by grabbing some rubber gloves from the medical chest, filling them with hot water in the kitchen, tying them off and bringing them back to nest them beneath the towels.

The room next to the main bedroom had been set up for the baby, and there she found soft cloth nappies, already washed and folded. One would do to dry the baby—better than a towel, which might not be as sterile as these new towelling squares.

'You've been busy,' Nick said, when, satisfied she had everything ready for the baby, she rejoined him at the bed.

'Best I could do but hopefully the plane will arrive with all the real gear, not makeshift stuff. Actually, isn't that a motor now?'

'That's Col,' Jane said, and began to cry in earnest, although now her cheeks were flushed and the tears were happy ones.

The tall, lanky young man strode into the room, dust clinging to his clothes and coating his skin.

'Janey!'

He threw himself onto his knees beside the bed and put his arms around his wife, his tears mingling with hers.

'Well, there goes my attempt to keep things sterile,'

Annabelle muttered to Nick. 'No way he won't want to hold the baby the moment he arrives.'

'I'll sort him out in a minute,' Nick assured her, 'and in the meantime, would you check what we've got in the obstetric pack as far as tubes for suctioning are concerned?'

'Obstetric pack, of course!' Annabelle said. 'I knew we had that—it probably has the things I need for wrapping up the baby.'

It did, but only a muslin wrap very like the sling she'd already found. But it also had tiny tubes for suctioning and a reminder list for checking Apgar scores. She readied what she'd need on the dressing table while Nick assured both parents that although the baby was premmie, it was within the range where there was every chance he or she would catch up with her peers by the time she was a year old. In the meantime, because they had to be very careful the baby didn't get an infection, would Col mind having a quick shower?

Poor Col looked panicstricken, but Jane assured him she'd needed his hug more than she'd needed him clean, and he dashed out of the room, returning clean and soap-smelling in time to hold the scrawny little scrap of humanity that dead-heated with his arrival.

Nick had handed the infant to Annabelle who suctioned both mouth and nose, juggling the tube as she simultaneously wrapped the cloth around the wet, squirming body.

Now, as the baby squawked indignantly, Annabelle gave it to Col, who lifted it close to Jane's face while both of them gazed in awe at their joint production.

'He's beautiful,' Col murmured, though Annabelle was reasonably sure the baby looked like nothing more than a skinned rabbit, and a remarkably unattractive one at that, all long dangly arms and legs, tiny squished face and bony rib cage.

'He's a she,' Jane said with a smile, unwrapping the bundle enough to see not only that detail but also to count fingers and toes.

Once Nick had helped Col cut the cord, Annabelle retrieved the infant, assuring both parents the baby would be fine but needed to be dried and kept warm. She didn't mention Apgar scores, but was relieved to find that although it had been a low five at birth it had risen to eight after the minute in which the parents had held the child.

'Okay?'

Nick was right behind her at the dressing table as she dried the infant and wrapped her in a clean cloth, then moved her from the dressing table to the makeshift crib, tucking the gloves full of hot water, wrapped in nappies, around the sides of the baby and adding another loose cover.

'That's the plane,' Col said. 'I turned on the lights before I came in. I'll drive out now and meet it. You want to come, Doc?'

Nick didn't want to go. He wanted to stand there and look at the tiny baby, born too soon but still with a good chance of growing up to lead a happy and healthy life.

More chance than his baby had been given.

He knew it was stupid to feel that way, but his gut was clenched into the tightest of knots, and even though he accompanied Col out of the room, his thoughts were in the past.

With typical efficiency, the RFDS staff whipped the baby into a proper humidicrib, the mother onto a stretcher and within twenty minutes of the plane landing, the pair were on their way to Brisbane, Col to follow in his car as soon as he'd sorted out caretaking for his animals.

'And drive safely,' were Jane's last words as she was loaded into the plane.

'You betcha!' Col replied, the earlier look of awe on his face now replaced by a smile an earthquake wouldn't move. 'That little girl needs a daddy!'

This was how families should be, Nick thought as he helped Annabelle clean up before heading for the troopie. It was how his family had been—his parents transparent in their love for him and their pride in all his achievements. Sometimes he'd wondered if it was because they hadn't been able to have more children that he'd been so well loved, but as he'd grown older, he'd realised that he'd been fortunate in that his parents' love for each other had been so strong and enduring that it had reached out and encapsulated him, making him think his marriage would be the same, his family a copy of the blueprint laid down by his parents.

# CHAPTER SIX

AWARE Nick had withdrawn into some place deep inside himself, Annabelle got behind the wheel of the troopie. She could drive slowly and watch for animals herself, leaving her companion to sort out whatever was bothering him without unnecessary conversation.

She sensed distress of some kind and, knowing pain herself, felt sorry for the man who, manlike, would probably not go blurting it out to a virtual stranger. Yet talking about Graham, even revealing only the bare bones of her one and only romantic entanglement, had somehow eased her pain, and maybe talking would help Nick.

Not that she'd ask. Not in a thousand years...

She slowed at the top of the jump-up, delighting in the view of the thin strip of gravel road stretching dead straight in front of them until it disappeared into the distance, flat, empty land either side of it, silver in the moonlight.

'It upset you, the baby being born so premmie?'

So much for a thousand years—it hadn't even been a thousand seconds!

She'd stopped the troopie as she'd asked the probably impertinent question and now she turned towards Nick, who was staring into the night.

'No!'

Okay, so you don't want to talk, Annabelle thought, and shifted into first gear, ready to take off again, but Nick's hand closed over hers.

'We're off the road,' he said quietly. 'Let's sit here for a while. It's very beautiful.'

It *was* very beautiful, but Annabelle was distracted from appreciating it by the fact that Nick had left his hand over hers on the gear lever. Of course, he'd probably forgotten it was there and it certainly meant nothing, but her body, which had at first started at the touch, was now, well, practically revelling in it.

How daft could one woman be? As if her experience with Graham hadn't been enough to warn her off men, particularly men like Nick Tempest with his love-'em-and-leave-'em reputation.

It was because she was needy—craving affection—craving a real family now Kitty was talking of moving in with her boyfriend. Oh, Annabelle knew all the psychology of it, but it didn't stop her body reacting to a man's touch.

Or was it just this man's touch?

She was so lost in her own mental musings that she missed the beginning of his conversation, catching up as he said, 'No idea she was pregnant, let alone that she'd had an abortion. There was a problem with some adhesions and the O and G chap she saw for the curette spoke to me about it without realising she hadn't told me about being pregnant in the first place, let alone what she'd done about it.'

The words were so bleakly matter-of-fact that the enormity of what he was saying took a moment to sink in.

'She had an abortion without telling you? Your wife? The model?'

Nick removed his hand from on top of the warm fingers on the gear lever and used it to rub the stubble on his chin.

'You're right, it was the model who had the abortion. Turned out she'd just received a fantastic offer from a top agency in New York and having a baby certainly didn't fit her career plan.'

He hadn't tried to hide the bitterness in his voice, but as he spoke he realised, probably for the first time, just how important that contract must have been to Nellie, and saw a faint glimpse of the situation from her side.

'Oh, Nick!'

The words were breathed into the cool night air then the owner of the warm fingers slid awkwardly across the bench seat of the troopie, lifting her legs to avoid the gear levers, and pressed against his side, putting her arms around him and hugging him to her.

'No wonder seeing the baby upset you. Why does love have to be so hard?'

She was comforting him, nothing more, yet his body was stirring as it hadn't stirred for ages.

Or had it stirred once before because of Annabelle?

Surely not!

If the gorgeous friends of Nellie's he'd been squiring to hospital and social functions hadn't stirred him, surely a pint-sized nurse with a cap of dark hair and nothing to recommend her apart from tantalising lips shouldn't be affecting his body in the slightest.

'I think it's all to do with timing, this love business,' the tantalising lips were saying. 'There I was with Kitty all grown up and in love herself, and I was desperate for a family—a family of my own—so it was easy to fall in love with a man who seemed like he'd make a good family man, little knowing the practice he'd already had.'

Nick wasn't sure if she was talking to comfort him, or to rid herself of a little more of her pain, but he didn't care because her chatter was soothing, and knowing she'd been hurt somehow brought her closer.

'And there's your Nellie, probably dreaming for years and years of hitting the big time and getting a New York agency. What do we give up for our dreams? That's the question. She gave up love, and hurt you in the process. All I gave up was my pride because I'd been so totally taken in, and if Graham's wife had known about me—or known he'd had someone on the side—then I probably hurt her too.'

Nick shifted so he could put his arm around Annabelle's shoulders and draw her closer.

'I can't imagine you ever hurting anyone,' he said quietly, and dropped a kiss on the cap of shiny hair, sniffing as he did so. Yep, rotten-egg gas, but he must be getting used to it.

'Not deliberately, but I don't think Nellie would have realised the extent of your hurt either. I don't think any of us set out to deliberately hurt someone else.'

She was silent for a moment before adding, 'Except, of course, people who cheat on their partners. They must *know* someone's going to get hurt. And what hurts most is the deceit—the fact that someone you love perhaps not lies to you but definitely isn't open and honest with you. It's betrayal.'

The pain was back in her voice as she repeated that damning word so it seemed only right to draw her closer and as she looked up at him, perhaps wondering at the embrace, it was inevitable that those lips would draw his to them, and that the kiss he hadn't given her the previous evening should be pressed on them right now.

She was tentative at first, he could feel it in the tension of her body and the slight trembling of her lips, but as he explored those lips with his, her mouth opened and her response brought heat thudding through his body.

No denying the stirring now...

Whatever had happened to control?

Annabelle's body snuggled closer to the warmth and strength of Nick's, though her head was yelling at her to stop at once, to cease and desist, to move away, drive back to Murrawalla and possibly move in with Eileen for the next two months.

Two days into the placement and she was practically in bed with Nick Tempest, the very last man in the world with whom she should be dallying.

Although now she knew about his marriage she could understand *his* dallying—why *would* he want to get seriously involved again?

But *she* wasn't a dallying kind of person—one experience had told her that. She couldn't handle dallying so she'd better stop kissing Nick right now!

Or soon!

Not immediately, but just soon enough she pushed away from Nick, lifting her legs over the gear levers as she slid back across the seat.

'It would really be totally stupid of us to get involved while we're out here,' she announced, putting the troopie into gear and taking off with a spray of gravel from under the wheels. 'I mean, it can't lead anywhere, and it would make life awkward when we go back to the

ER, and people here would talk, although that part of it wouldn't worry me—people'd just say, *She's like her old man.*'

Now there was bitterness in *her* voice, a tone Nick was sure was foreign to her. Mind you, he wasn't thinking quite straight, still trying to sort out why Annabelle pulling out of their kiss had upset him so much. As she'd said, it would be stupid for them to get involved.

Wouldn't it?

He couldn't answer that so he thought about what she'd said.

'Your old man? Your father? What would our having an affair have to do with him? Would he be upset?'

His companion gave a laugh that had no humour in it.

'If my dad's on a seam of opal you and I could make love right in front of him and he wouldn't notice, not that he's noticed anything in my life for the last six years. No, the town would say I'm like him because he always had a woman in his life, many, many women, some he married and some he didn't. There'd be plenty of wise heads nodding and making "the apple doesn't fall far from the tree" remarks if you and I got involved out here.'

Raw pain grated in every word and it was all Nick could do not to slide across the seat as she'd done earlier, and take her in his arms. Except she was driving and they'd probably have an accident and, anyway, shouldn't he be watching for animals on the road?

Was it the darkness and the emptiness of the land that had them both spilling out things they'd probably not shared with anyone before? He'd certainly never told anyone about Nellie and the abortion, not even his parents. And he'd certainly never heard any talk in the ER about Annabelle, although perhaps she'd moved hospitals four months ago to get away from the rat who'd hurt her and no one in the ER knew the story.

She was slowing the car and, peering ahead, he could just make out a dark shadow on the road.

'Wombat,' she said, stopping altogether, putting the car into neutral and dragging on the handbrake. 'Come on, you don't get to see a wombat often. Let's say hello.'

Her voice told him she'd recovered from the angst of earlier and he was so happy to hear her happy again that he opened the door and dropped down onto the dusty road, coming cautiously around the front of the vehicle to see the big, cumbersome animal lumbering across the road.

Annabelle joined him and it seemed only natural to take her hand so they could follow the wombat into some scrubby bushes on the other side of the road.

'There's so much good stuff in the world,' she announced as the wombat wandered on about his business and they returned to the car, 'that it's impossible to brood over the bad stuff for long. I'm sorry I dumped all that on you. I'm really over it now—except for Dad, of course, but I'll sort him out while I'm here.'

Nick opened the car door for her, thinking of the bits and pieces of her life she'd revealed. No doubt her father's parade of women meant she'd never had a decent family life, which would be why she longed for a family for herself.

On top of which, she'd be very cautious going into a relationship, not wanting to mirror her father's behaviour by going from man to man.

He shut the door but couldn't shut away his thoughts, wondering just what else he might learn about this woman in the time they'd spend together. Given what they'd covered in two days, he guessed they'd have no secrets left at all after two months.

Although the circumstances they'd found themselves in had prompted both their confessions about hurt in the past, and they'd be unlikely to encounter more situations like those two…

She shouldn't have taken his hand. Annabelle could still feel the strength of his fingers against hers, the heat of his skin—no, she definitely shouldn't have taken his hand.

He'd probably read something into it beyond a desire to share the thrill of seeing a wombat in the wild.

She'd have to be careful in the future—no touching, not even getting near the man—for her body was behaving erratically, probably because she was anxious about the reunion with her father.

Annabelle's thoughts raced as erratically as her body was behaving, switching from one thing to another, all the while avoiding the big issue, the fact that she'd kissed Nick.

Not only kissed him, but enjoyed the kiss and, worse, shown her enjoyment.

What was *wrong* with her?

Was it nothing more than a simple craving for physical affection?

No way!

She wasn't going down that track!

Her father had given in to his physical cravings for years and all his kids were probably damaged in some way.

Not that she considered herself damaged, but she'd certainly gone into her relationship with Graham far too quickly and easily, mistaking physical attraction for love.

'Lights of home!'

Nick's voice brought her out of her aggravating thoughts but she wished he hadn't used the word 'home', for all that it was said jokingly.

'The wild metropolis of Murrawalla.' She knew she had to respond in kind. She'd already told this man far too much about herself, and now had to retreat and put a decent distance between them.

'Do you want to stop at the transport café for a coffee or a snack or shall we go straight to the house?'

There, that was good! Common-sense conversation and no silly wobble in her voice.

'I think back to the house. Second late night in a row. I hope this is an aberration rather than a regular thing.'

'I think it would be,' Annabelle replied, but the stiltedness of the conversation made her feel uncomfortable. Just when they'd got rid of the false intimacy thing they'd found themselves discomfort instead—all because of a kiss that had really been nothing more than sympathy.

Well, not much more!

Nick headed straight for the shower when they reached home, and Annabelle prepared for bed. It was after midnight and they had to leave at seven in the morning to drive out to the drilling site. Heading for the bathroom to clean her teeth, she passed Nick, a towel sarong-style round his waist, and the sight of his bare chest with firm muscles and a sprinkle of dark hair stirred her body once again.

Could he read her thoughts that he grinned at her and said, 'You can look but not touch, unless you want to reconsider the possibility of a short romance?'

She studied him for a moment, trying to read a face that told her nothing.

'Would *you* like that?' she asked, and now he did react, looking shocked then puzzled, before finally shaking his head.

'I honestly don't know,' he eventually answered. 'The very last thing I expected when I came out here was to be attracted to the nurse half of the team—attracted to anyone—but I can't deny that something's flared up between us. Maybe it happens to all the people who come out here and it's something I'll have to take into account when choosing people to come. Maybe it's something in the water!'

He smiled at her, and reached out to ruffle her hair.

'The smelly water,' he added lightly, before walking into his bedroom and closing the door behind him.

Trying desperately to not think about him dropping that towel or wondering what, if anything, he wore to bed, Annabelle scrubbed her teeth with unnecessary force, rinsed out her mouth, washed her face and hurried to her own bedroom.

Where she lay awake for what seemed like hours, arguing with herself about the advisability or otherwise of a brief affair.

'I don't think I'm an affair kind of person, and not entirely because of my father's lack of commitment to any one woman.'

Her midnight cogitations had obviously stayed in her

mind because she blurted that out to Nick at breakfast the next morning.

'Probably just as well,' he said.

This puzzled Annabelle enough that she had to ask.

'What's probably just as well? You're not interested in an affair with me? I don't measure up to your standards?' She thought about that for a moment, remembering pictures she'd seen in the paper of Nick squiring very beautiful women to different functions. Of course she wouldn't measure up.

But just as she began to feel annoyed with him, the grin she was beginning to love lightened his face once again, and he poured milk over his cereal before replying.

'If there's one thing I've finally learned from my marital and near-marital disasters, it's not to rush into things.'

Fair enough. She should have learnt that too but...

'Near-marital disasters—you had more than one?'

He smiled again but there was a far-away look in his eyes as he tackled his cereal, nearly finishing the bowl before speaking once again.

'I grew up in a working-class family with what I suppose are old-fashioned working-class morals. I met a girl when I finished high school and got engaged to her when we both started university because that was what I thought was the right thing to do once we'd started sleeping together. She was at the conservatorium and did a tour with their orchestra and ended up falling in love with the second violin—'

'*Second* violin? Not even the first?' Annabelle teased, although she'd felt a pang of longing when he'd talked of engagements and 'right things to do', evidence of a moral compass he'd obviously got from his family.

'You can laugh!' Nick told her crossly. 'I was devastated at the time, although later I realised it was best for both of us. We were totally unsuited to each other and far too young at twenty to be thinking of lifetime commitments.'

'And since then? Did you still get engaged to everyone you slept with?'

No grin this time, but a distinct growl.

'It's the intimacy thing again isn't it?' he complained. 'Just because we're living together, we don't have to know every detail of each other's lives, and if there's one thing I *don't* do, Annabelle Donne, it's kiss and tell! For all that I've already told you more about my life than anyone else in the universe, that's it—no more heart-to-hearts, no more confessions. We're two professionals out here to do a job, so let's start behaving that way.'

The frown on his face and the anger in his eyes told Annabelle he was serious. This was the man they called Storm back in the ER, coldly professional, personally polite, but always a little aloof.

Now he was using that persona to push her away and for all it was a good thing, given how she was beginning to feel about him, the Nick she'd been getting to know would have been a lot easier companion to have around for the next two months.

Could she ease Nick back out from behind his Storm cover?

'You're right, of course,' she assured him, keeping her voice teasingly light, although inside she was feeling tense—the way she'd always felt in the ER when he'd been around. 'And you certainly shouldn't kiss and tell but I was thinking our talking about things is actually like a kind of group therapy but with only two people. Probably do us both the world of good.'

'What would do us the world of good is getting on the road,' Nick told her, determined not to be dragged into any more intimacy with this witch of a woman who'd already had him revealing stuff he hadn't told anyone before. 'Shall we take Bruce? He got upset when we went without him last night.'

The trip to the drilling site was uneventful, as was the rest of the week. Until Friday. Nick was watching his toast, a totally unnecessary task as the toaster was automatic and the toast always bobbed up a beautiful, even, golden colour, just how he liked it.

But watching the toast meant he didn't have to sit at the breakfast bar beside Annabelle, who was munching her way through a huge bowl of cereal and turning the pages of a book far too often to be really reading it.

So far she hadn't brought the book with her to the dinner table, although some evenings the conversation between them had been so stilted he'd rather wished she had. This had been the pattern of their days since Tuesday morning when he'd virtually put discussions of his love-life—either of their love-lives—off limits.

Which was where they should be, he reminded himself as he rescued the toast and slathered it with butter, then coated it with the delicious lemon butter Annabelle had made one evening.

And it wasn't that they didn't talk at all. There were always patients to discuss and new things for him to learn, unusual accidents to attend—not many ER doctors had patients with a gore wound from a bull—but the colleagues-only atmosphere between them was beginning to wear thin as far as he was concerned, though, heaven knew, he didn't want to go back to the intimacy.

'You guys decent?'

Eileen announced her presence only seconds before she came through the door and Nick realised she must have known they'd be decent—know nothing was going on between them. Hell, the whole town would, so polite were they to each other.

Which was what he wanted, wasn't it?

'You remember it's the B and S tomorrow night?' Eileen asked. 'Bob Cartwright—it's on his property,' she added in an aside to Nick, 'wondered if you'd like to come out today instead of tomorrow and do a spot of pig shooting tonight. Seems he remembers you as a great spotter, Annabelle.'

Spotter? More foreign language, Nick was thinking, but he was watching Annabelle's face and saw it light up in a way it hadn't for days—sheer excitement illuminating it from within.

'Oh, wouldn't it be great,' she breathed, then she shook her head. 'And totally irresponsible,' she added. 'The ute jolts and I fall and break my collarbone—great help that would be to the people out here who need a two-armed nurse. No, Eileen, tell Bob to count me out, but Nick could go in one of the utes if he wants to see the fun.'

Nick had to admit he was intrigued, but more by the words he'd heard than the thought of going on a pig shoot.

'What's a spotter?'

Annabelle grinned at him for probably the first time

in days and he felt that silly shift inside his chest—only because they were friends again, he was sure.

'The utes have big spotlights mounted between the headlights and another one or two on the top of the cabins, and the spotter stands on the tray at the back, moving the top spotlights until he picks up the movement of animals, then the ute closes in and the spotter has to identify them as pigs.'

Nick pictured the scene.

'After which the guy driving the ute charges after them and a number of people all with guns and probably unsecured by seat belts start firing live ammunition into the air,' he guessed. 'And you're worried the worst that can happen to you is a broken collarbone?'

'It's not that dangerous. The shooters are sensible enough—most of the time—and feral pigs are a terrible nuisance. They destroy so much vegetation they make it hard for even the kangaroos to survive. And the wombats!'

She added the last with such defiance Nick had to smile.

'You don't have to defend country people to me, Annabelle,' he said. 'Even in a week I've seen enough to have enormous admiration for their resilience, work ethic and stoicism not to criticise them, even if I had the right. But, no, Eileen, I'd just as soon not join the pig shoot, but please thank whoever it was who invited us.'

'Invited me, mainly,' Annabelle reminded him, and Nick laughed. This was the tetchy, mouthy young woman he'd got to know on the plane and in their first few days in Murrawalla and he was pleased to have her back, for all the discomfort that would cause in his body, which didn't seem to understand an attraction to her was off limits.

'That's okay,' Eileen said, 'I'll let Bob know. He also asked if you'd like to sleep up at the house but he did say to warn you it probably won't be much quieter up there—his boys have a lot of friends staying.'

'Stay in the house and have Nick miss out on a night sleeping under the stars?' Annabelle demanded, while the delight on her face suggested the 'sleeping out under the stars' wasn't going to be quite the thrill she made out it would be.

Nick toyed with the idea of accepting the invitation to sleep in the house—in a bed rather than the swag he'd unrolled and examined but had yet to use, and away from the woman whose body was tormenting his—but he guessed Annabelle was waiting for him to chicken out and he shook his head.

'No, I've been looking forward to sleeping under the stars for weeks,' he told Eileen.

'What a lie!' Annabelle pounced the moment Eileen left the house. 'You didn't even know about the B and S until you were on the plane.'

'But Eileen didn't know that and I wanted the re-fusal to sound polite,' Nick countered, then, because they were really talking again, he added, 'Did you really ride around on the back of utes spotting wild pigs when you were younger?'

She found a smile but it definitely wasn't one of her best efforts.

'I did, but it seems so long ago—another world...'

He knew the conversation should end there. Told him-self if she'd wanted him to know more she'd have kept talking, but the not sadness but nostalgia in her voice had got to him, and on top of that, now he had the old Annabelle back he didn't want her reverting to the polite nurse-colleague she'd been for the last few days.

*For all that he'd been the one who'd pushed them back that way!*

'Tell me about it.'

Annabelle hesitated. The days since they'd decided to back away from all personal stuff had been awkward, but awkward was better than being close without really being close.

She knew that didn't make much sense but deep inside she knew the further she could detach herself from Nick, the safer her heart would be.

So wouldn't telling him about spotting—revealing only this tiny part of her past—leave her heart open to attack again, open it to the jeopardy of love?

Of course not! She was being stupid.

'Of course, if you don't want to tell me, that's okay too,' he was saying. 'Perhaps we should discuss the arrangements we have to make for the ball itself. Do we have to dress?'

'Clean shirt and trousers for you, but I'll dress. All the girls do, though I'm hardly a girl, and the spotting thing was nothing much.'

She paused, wondering if Nick would push it, but suddenly the memory was so vivid—the night, the lights, the shouts, the smell of gunpowder—it came rushing out.

'The young jackaroos on the property where Dad has his mine would organise a pig shoot now and then, but to them it was an excuse to have a few beers and, yes, I know alcohol and guns don't mix but at thirteen I wasn't really aware of the dangers. Anyway, they used to use me as a spotter and I loved it, driving over the country in the moonlight, no roads, no boundaries, there was something so—so elemental somehow about it. Sometimes I even drove the ute, usually to take them back to the homestead. They hardly ever killed anything but I guess when you're stuck in the middle of nowhere and rarely see a soul other than your father and sister and whatever woman was in Dad's life at the time, anything would be exciting.'

She pushed away from the breakfast bar, her cereal unfinished, her stomach churning as more memories stirred. The last time she'd returned to the mine after a pig shoot, her mother had been there, a court order in her hand, giving her custody of daughters she hadn't seen for seven years and had rarely contacted in that time.

Annabelle's protests to her father had gone unanswered. Oh, he'd promised to always be there for them—to watch over them from afar—but at the time it had seemed to Annabelle that he was happy to be rid of them. In fact, Kitty had told her later, he had helped to pack up their clothes. The betrayal had cut so deep that hate had tried to enter where love had been, but the love had been too strong, so all Annabelle had been able to do was ignore the hurt and continue to protect Kitty as best she could.

'Annabelle?'

Had Nick sensed the shift in her mood that he called after her as she sought refuge in her bedroom, the memories so vivid she could feel the gut-wrenching pain all over again.

'I'll be right back,' she managed, but she knew she wouldn't be. She flung herself down on the bed and cried as she hadn't cried before—not when Graham had revealed his deceit, not when their mother had dumped her and Kitty, not even when Kitty had announced she was moving in with Joe.

She wasn't even sure why she was crying.

For the loss of a simple life she'd once known?

Or for the loss of her father's love?

# CHAPTER SEVEN

'SO, WHAT do we need to take?'

Somehow she'd recovered enough to do the Friday morning clinic at the hospital, and if Nick had noticed her red puffy eyes he'd had enough sense not to comment. Now their first week in Murrawalla was behind them and officially they were off duty, or as off duty as a country doctor ever was.

'We'll be fed and fed well,' Annabelle told him, 'and alcohol will flow very freely. We'll have the big first-aid kit in the troopie for any emergency patching up we need to do, but breakfast will be steak and eggs, and if you feel you won't be able to face that after an interrupted night's sleep, we can take our own cereal. Plenty of water—I like to know where my drinking water is coming from and if we have to rehydrate some hungover young men and women, at least we'll have clean water. I'll make sure there are some electrolyte tablets in the first-aid kit, and plenty of paracetamol for headaches.'

'What is it we're going to? An orgy?'

'I do hope not,' Annabelle told him. 'And being at the Cartwrights', I would guess it will be fairly well supervised, but stories of what goes on at B and S balls are legion so we'd better be prepared.'

* * *

But nothing could have prepared Nick for the scene that met his eyes as he stopped the troopie beyond the first ring of utes near a huge barn on the Cartwrights' property.

He'd driven because one look at his colleague as she'd come out of her bedroom in a long black gown of shiny satin and high-heeled silver sandals that matched an elaborate silver necklace round her neck had told him that if he didn't take the wheel, he'd spend the whole drive staring at her.

'Stupid, isn't it?' she'd said, twirling around in front of him. 'But the girls and women do dress up, besides which last time I saw the Cartwright boys I was thirteen and looked eight and they treated me like a kid brother. I think I deserve to show them I've grown up.'

Nick had swallowed hard. He'd been stunned before she'd twirled around, but the twirl had made the dress move against her body—a far more voluptuous body than her everyday attire of check shirt and jeans had ever hinted at.

'Here do to park?' he asked, still trying not to look at her, although he couldn't entirely ignore her presence for tonight she smelt of roses, not rotten eggs.

Clean, fresh roses—just cut. Not that he knew much about roses, just cut or otherwise…

'Here's fine,' she said, then turned to Bruce, who was already whimpering with excitement at being able to meet up with so many of his dog friends. 'As for you, make sure you behave yourself. No taking food off a plate even if it's on the ground, no fights, and be back at the troopie by midnight.'

'Or he'll turn into a pumpkin?' Nick said, desperate

to break the tension he'd been feeling since he'd set eyes on his transformed companion.

'Something like that,' Annabelle replied. 'Would you open the back door and let him out? He's likely to jump on me and I'd like to stay clean for a little longer. Would you also drag out the swags and spread them by the far side of the troopie so we've marked our territory? Eileen put in a few folding chairs as well, so we should set them up on the near side so if we do have a patient, we can sit him or her down.'

She was fiddling with a box she'd put on the seat between them and now pulled out a long fluorescent light, the lead of which she inserted into the cigarette lighter.

'That runs off the auxiliary battery so it won't flatten the main battery, not that these things pull much power.'

She hooked it up on the roof rack of the troopie and turned on the light, illuminating the area where Nick had set out the chairs and a small folding table.

'Looks like a setting for a night picnic,' he said, risking a glance at his transformed companion.

Beautiful—she was beautiful. From the top of her shining cap of hair to the tips of her silver-painted toenails, although he guessed the toes were already a little dusty.

'What now?' he asked, as she switched off the light so the light from the barn and the fires burning outside seemed brighter.

'We go and introduce ourselves and then we mingle. We really don't have much to do at this stage, so enjoy your dinner then dance if you feel like it. Actually, you'll be lucky to finish your dinner before someone whisks you away for a dance. A lot of the country lads won't dance at all and most won't show their paces until they've had a few drinks, so male partners are always in demand.'

She led the way to the barn, where Eileen was already installed at one of the tables reserved for the more sedate members of the party—parents, friends and relatives who would eat then depart, leaving the young people to party. Eileen introduced them around, and Nick saw the surprise on many faces as they worked out who Annabelle was. Had she not been home since she was thirteen?

And if not, why not? Even in divorce situations most fathers continued to see their children.

Or didn't they?

He remembered some statistics he'd once read and felt a surge of sympathy for the smiling woman who was dazzling the company in her slinky black dress.

The barn had been decorated with balloons and streamers, while bales of hay placed all around the walls provided somewhere to sit—if you didn't mind the prickliness of the seating. Nick was surprised to see uniformed security people here and there around the crowd but before he could ask Annabelle about them his attention was claimed by one of the hosts.

'Have your dinner then we'll dance.' Mrs Cartwright handed him a plate loaded with meat and vegetables and pointed to a spare seat at the table. 'It's ages since I had a handsome young doctor to dance with.'

She wasn't flirting, Nick knew that, simply making him feel at home in this strange environment, so he took the seat she offered him, and as he ate he listened to the conversation going on around him—rail transport apparently caused less bruising for cattle than trucking them to market, live export of cattle was growing all the time, shearing teams were becoming scarcer, should the locals who had sheep start training up their jackaroos to shear as well?

'It must seem like double-Dutch to you,' Mrs Cartwright said, and Nick had to admit he had trouble following some of it.

'But I'm finding myself more and more ashamed of how little I know about my own country. I've been to New York and Paris, but never been far west of Brisbane. It's been a revelation.'

'At least you're not too proud to admit it,' his other neighbour, an elderly man with a huge white moustache, said. 'We've had young fellows out here thought they knew the lot and they're the kind that get into trouble. They don't take the time to learn and don't bother to listen to the locals. This place, like all country towns, needs a doctor, and we're grateful to the drilling company for this arrangement. But once the drillers go, what happens?'

Nick was suddenly aware of Annabelle watching him from across the table. She must have caught the end of the conversation and was listening for his reply. Not that he could tell the elderly gent that there were tentative plans to close down the nurse-doctor service even before the drillers finished.

'It's a problem in most country areas,' he said, aware he was wimping out but unable to discuss the options the mining company was considering. Yet the answer caused more than a twinge of guilt, for he was holding back from Annabelle as well, and something in her face told him she suspected his answer was an evasion.

Fortunately, seeing he'd finished his dinner, Mrs Cartwright claimed him for a dance, which led to other, mostly younger women demanding that they too wanted to dance with the doc. Not that Annabelle was missing out on the exercise, constantly whirling past him in the arms of some young buck, or gyrating on the edge of the crowd with a be-jeaned and cowboy-hatted youth. Presumably these partners had partaken of the necessary Dutch courage, which prompted Nick to keep a close eye on them.

And her...

But when he found her between sets and suggested a dance, she shook her head.

'Oh, I don't think so, do you?' she said, smiling at him in such an innocent way he wanted to take her in his arms and hold her close and *make* her dance with him.

Yelps and barks and encouraging shouts diverted him, especially as Annabelle, ballgown hitched up in one hand, already had a head start on him towards the sounds of the melee. Whether it had started with two young men fighting, Nick didn't know, but now about eight were involved, all throwing wild punches.

Once again Nick found himself lifting the nurse half of his team out of the fray, this time setting her down in the back of the nearest ute.

'And stay there!' he ordered as he joined some other more-or-less sober men in separating the combatants.

No one appeared badly hurt or, if they were, they were too macho to admit it, so once things had settled down, the most inebriated of the young men was taken to a trough of water where he was ordered to dunk his head and sober up by one of the security team.

Certain things were under control, Nick turned to lift Annabelle back to the ground but she was already in the arms of a tall, thin streak of a cowboy, who was holding her far too intimately and saying something that made her laugh out loud.

'One of the Cartwright boys,' she said, when she'd detached herself from the young man and rejoined Nick. 'It's after midnight. Have you had enough fun and frivolity? If so, we can go and sit by the troopie and watch from afar, ready if we're needed to provide some assistance.'

Yes, he'd had enough of the fun and frivolity. One group of young people was now doing the limbo, lithe bodies bending backwards to work their way under what looked like a thin metal fence post. But what he would have liked was to dance with Annabelle, to feel her body against his as it had been when he'd lifted her onto the back of the ute.

Not that he'd ask again. She'd been fairly firm in her refusal the first time.

Although had she?

I don't think so. That was all she'd said.

The music was loud enough for them to hear it from over where they were, quite close to the troopie, so he turned to her and held out his arms.

'Just one dance,' he said, and when she didn't argue he drew her close and they twirled slowly around on the rough red earth, beneath a shimmering canopy of stars.

Nothing went on for ever, Annabelle reminded herself as soon as the silly wish that this might whispered in her heart. But even knowing that, she remained in Nick's arms, allowing him to turn her to the music, following his lead, although now they were barely moving, more embracing, body to body, warmth and desire flickering between them, taunting them—well, her anyway. She had no idea how Nick was feeling.

He drew her closer and she had to amend that thought as well. She had *some* idea of how he was feeling…

'I hate him, I hate him, I'm going to kill him and how will I get home?'

The hysterical cries broke them apart, Nick recovering first, setting Annabelle back against the troopie before turning to face whatever new drama was coming their way.

And whatever it was, even though it sounded like a girl or very young woman, he'd put himself between Annabelle and the danger, if there was danger, and Annabelle felt a warmth she shouldn't feel at his protective behaviour.

Not that she could stay there. It *was* a young woman—a girl-woman, Annabelle suspected—probably little more than seventeen, tears and make-up streaking unattractively down her face. Even then she was beautiful, tall and slender, long blonde hair carefully straightened to fall like a curtain down her back.

Nick already had an arm around the newcomer's shoulders and was speaking to her in soothing tones. Annabelle joined them, taking the girl's hands and leading her to a chair. The moonlight and lights from the barn and fire were bright enough for them to see she wasn't injured so she left their bright light off and knelt in front of the sobbing girl.

'What's happened?' she asked gently, but the girl could only wail, eventually flinging her arms around

Nick's waist—he'd been standing by the chair—and
declaring that she wished she was dead.

Annabelle got up and fetched a glass of water, handing it to Nick before returning to the back of the troopie
where she found the little gas stove and started water
boiling for a cup of tea. Nothing like a cuppa—although
most young people she knew lived on coffee and sports
drinks.

She returned with the tea but Nick hadn't made much
progress with their 'patient', who was still clinging to
him and sobbing all over his good trousers. Probably
streaking them with eyeshadow and mascara as well.

The cattiness of the thought made Annabelle feel
ashamed, but only momentarily because when she eased
the girl away from Nick and offered her the tea, the
ungrateful brat threw it on the ground and demanded a
shot of vodka.

'Not part of our medical kit,' Annabelle told her, picking up the plastic mug and wincing as she saw she now
had tea-mud on her silver sandals. Not that they'd have
been good for anything after an evening out here, which
was why she'd bought a cheap pair, but this girl—

'Tell us the problem.'

Nick now squatted in front of her, holding her hands
and speaking firmly. Annabelle would have liked nothing more than to have walked away—after all, he'd had
enough tall beautiful blondes in his life to be able to
handle them. But propriety meant she had to stay with
the pair. It would be only too easy for a vindictive young
woman to accuse a man of impropriety and though it
was unlikely, Annabelle wasn't going to leave, just in
case!

Haltingly, the girl told her story. She'd returned,

probably none too sober, although she didn't admit that, to where she and her boyfriend had left their big swag, only to find some other girl in it with him.

'Maybe you mistook the swag,' Nick suggested. 'They all look the same to me.'

'It was in the back of Jack's ute,' the girl told him. 'I wouldn't mistake that. And they weren't just lying there, I could tell.'

The tears flowed freely once again, and Annabelle fetched a small blanket from the back of the troopie and wrapped it around the girl.

'Come on,' she said, as gently as she could, given the girl had ruined the sandals. 'I'll take you up to the house. Mrs Cartwright will find you a bed.'

The girl wrenched violently away and threw her arms around Nick once again.

'I can't go there. The Cartwrights are his cousins— they'll think it's a great joke. I hate him, I hate him, I hate him.'

Nick was holding the girl and looking helplessly at Annabelle, who realised they were now stuck with the distraught stranger.

'We've got a spare swag, she can have that.' Annabelle marched round to the back of the troopie once again and hauled out the swag that would have been hers had she not brought her own.

Unrolling it, she sniffed at the sleeping bag inside— a faint perfume told her it had been used by a woman so presumably it was reasonably clean. She dragged it round the side to where their two swags were unrolled, Bruce already quite comfortable on hers, and put the third one down beside it.

'Come on,' she said, approaching the girl once again. 'You can stay here with us.'

'Her name's Melody,' Nick told her, gently urging the girl forward, almost carrying her round the big vehicle. 'There,' he said when they reached the swags. 'You've even got our good dog Bruce for company.'

Melody, it turned out, hated dogs, and how could she possibly sleep on the outside where wild animals might get her? So with gritted teeth Annabelle reorganised the sleeping arrangements so Melody would be tucked in next to Nick, Annabelle on her other side, while poor Bruce was banished to the troopie.

Biting back various sarcastic remarks she wanted to make, Annabelle used a warm, wet cloth to clean the make-up off Melody's face, gave up her own warm pyjamas for the girl to sleep in, and generally nursemaided her into the swag, even preparing a cup of warm milk and honey when the girl complained she'd never be able to sleep.

'The stars *are* beautiful.' It was much later when Annabelle heard Nick's voice above the faint snuffling sounds of Melody's deep sleep.

'They are,' she agreed, and wished with all her heart that she was lying closer to him, if only so they could touch each other's hands and share the magic of the night.

It was a foolish wish, and definitely not one she could share with the main who lay beneath the stars, with her, yet not with her. So instead she thought about what she knew of him. Two serious relationships, both of them disasters. No wonder he went from woman to woman these days, permanence the last thing on his mind. It was as she'd sensed from first seeing him in the ER. He was the last man she should be attracted to, although now she knew the reason for his lack of commitment to one woman, she could understand his behaviour.

Understanding, however, didn't make him a suitable candidate for loving. A commitment-phobe was the last man in the world for someone who wanted permanence—who wanted a family.

'That was a big sigh.'

Nick's voice, coming again out of the darkness, seemed to add emphasis to her thoughts.

'Deep-breathing exercises,' Annabelle told him, ignoring the ripple of awareness his voice had started in her body. 'Helps me go to sleep.'

'I doubt anything will help me sleep,' Nick responded. 'There's a stone the size of a brick under my left buttock, and another one where my pillow would be if I was back in civilisation in a bed. That said, I can think of something that could take my mind off the rocks and stones. Didn't Melody say something about people sharing swags?'

Desire sizzled through Annabelle's body, and all the reasons for not getting involved with Nick were wiped from her mind. Fortunately, there were other issues involved.

'You can get double swags,' she told him. 'Ours are definitely single. Besides, how would poor Melody feel, already deserted by her boyfriend, if she woke up to find her saviour, you, had someone in *his* swag.'

Nick smiled up at the stars. He loved the way Annabelle argued things out, especially as he knew she was arguing against herself as much as against him. The physical attraction that had flared between them had been totally unexpected, but it was no less real for that.

And keeping a polite distance and sticking to colleague-type conversation wasn't dampening it, so it was almost inevitable that some time over the next two months they'd end up in bed together.

*That* thought wiped the smile off his face.

Even in a week he knew enough about Annabelle to know she wouldn't go into any relationship without one hundred per cent commitment, which made him the very last person on earth with whom she should have an affair.

There was, of course, the possibility that their time out here would be cut short. Should he push for that to happen?

Now he was frowning at the stars as he sorted through conflicting emotions. Staying would give him time to learn more about the area and life out here, something he found himself wanting to do, but going would remove the temptation bound up in Annabelle's compact but shapely body.

There was also a slight niggle in the back of his mind that not sharing what he knew about the drilling company's plans with Annabelle was—well, not exactly deceitful but a bit off somehow. It was a work matter and they were work partners and for that reason he should have told her, but the company rep who'd outlined the alternative plans had warned him, Nick, to keep quiet about it, so he had...

He shifted so the rock was under his hip, and the one where his pillow should be was no longer squashing his ear. Sleeping under the stars was all very well and good, but surely a blow-up mattress could be included in these swags!

To ward off the discomfort, he turned his thoughts

back to Annabelle, no doubt sleeping soundly just a yard away. He imagined how a double swag would work, and where he could tuck her body so they touched skin to skin as much as possible.

Bad idea, thinking such thoughts, but he wasn't totally surprised to wake in the dim light of pre-dawn to find her standing over him, fully dressed in her usual attire of jeans and shirt, no skin visible at all except for her face, which wore an angry scowl.

'Madam Melody would like to leave now, right now, as she doesn't want to face the boyfriend, and when we get to Murrawalla, apparently she can phone Daddy and he'll send a plane to fetch her home to Sydney. Maybe send someone to shoot the boyfriend as well, though I think she might have made that bit up.'

Nick eased himself stiffly into a sitting position, and cautiously moved his shoulders, surprised to find he was less sore than he'd thought he'd be. He was preparing to slide out of the swag when he remembered he'd taken off his trousers and as his briefs were very brief and as his dreams had been of Annabelle, maybe he'd better wait until she wasn't looming over him.

'I'll be right with you,' he said, 'but any chance of a cuppa before we set off?'

The scowl on Annabelle's face deepened.

'You're only getting it because the water in the billy should still be hot. Madam needed tea at two a.m. and again at four. She also had to throw up three times and cry another seven, and for someone who's never slept on the ground before, it seems to me you slept particularly soundly.'

With that she huffed away, leaving Nick to emerge from his cocoon with a smile on his face. He *did* feel sorry that Annabelle had had to cope with the girl on her own. Hell, he'd even drive so his colleague could snooze on the way back to town, but what pleased him most of all was that he *had* slept. He'd lain on the stony, lumpy ground with a bit of canvas under him and above him a sleeping bag, and had slept so deeply that the partying in the distance and the disturbances right beside him hadn't bothered him in the slightest.

He pulled on his trousers, grabbed his toilet bag and a mug of water and headed for the bushes beyond their camp. Morning ablutions in the bush! He breathed in the clean, cold air, and looked in admiration at the colours striping the sky to the east. This was a world that had never, for some reason, interested him—had never captured his imagination enough for him to want to explore it. But he was beginning to see how it could seep into a person's soul, and he knew he'd be spending more time exploring the Outback in the future.

With whom?

The inner question came from nowhere.

Not one of the lovely blondes he usually spent leisure time with, that was for sure. Nellie's reaction to something as simple as a drive up the mountains had always been a deep groan.

'Fresh air, Nick,' she used to say. 'It could kill us—and the sun! Let's shop instead...'

'Come *on*!'

The young Nellie clone was leaning back against the troopie in a pair of pyjamas with teddy bears all over them. They *had* to be Annabelle's, although he'd only seen her in a baggy T-shirt in the mornings.

He raised his eyebrows at her as she handed him

a mug of tea and nodded at the pyjama-clad young woman.

'My sister gave them to me,' Annabelle said defensively. 'And I brought them with me because I hate sleeping in my clothes but I suspected we—or *one* of us—might have to get up in the night to tend to people and at least I'd be decent.'

'And ever so cute,' Nick told her, then regretted the teasing remark as colour rose in her face.

'*She* might be cute, but all I am is dirty, rumpled, smelling of sick and very tired, so don't start with the smart remarks.'

She turned away to call Bruce, who ambled over with an uncooked sausage in his mouth.

'Now we *have* to leave,' Annabelle added, 'before whoever's cooking breakfast finds out Bruce has been at the supplies.'

She opened the car door and waved for Melody to get in.

'Oh, I can't sit in the middle, I'll get carsick,' their visitor said.

'Of course you would,' Annabelle muttered, hitching herself up and sliding across the seat, carefully putting her legs so one was each side of the gear lever, an arrangement that meant Nick brushed against her right knee every time he changed gear.

But brushing her knee was nothing to the effect her body pressed against his in the cramped front seat had on his nerves, which all leapt to attention and kept suggesting body-pressing of another kind—the kind he'd been considering when he'd slipped into sleep the previous night.

Maybe he could last a month in close proximity

to Annabelle without absolutely *having* to make love to her.

*Perhaps!*

And the placement was two months...

Surely he had more willpower than this!

Surely if he just stopped thinking about it...

Melody was prattling on about the boyfriend and her father and planes and killing people—the girl definitely had murder on her mind.

'You really shouldn't talk that way,' Annabelle told her. 'What if Jack had an accident on the way home and was killed, wouldn't you feel bad?'

'No, I wouldn't,' Melody declared. 'It would serve him right.'

'No, it wouldn't.' Nick could feel the tension growing in Annabelle's body as she answered the spoilt young woman. 'No one deserves to die before their time, especially not young men and women. That's why road statistics are so tragic. You come and visit the ER some time and see people dying and maybe then you won't use words like *kill* and *die* so easily.'

'They're only words,' Melody muttered, but Nick had a feeling maybe something of what Annabelle had said had got through the self-centred young woman's head, particularly as she began to cry again, this time in a helpless, despairing kind of way.

Annabelle switched immediately from critic to comforter, holding the weeping Melody in her arms and murmuring soothingly to her.

'You've got to look on the good side of this,' Annabelle said when Melody finally stopped weeping. 'Now you know Jack's a rat, you can get out and find yourself someone else, someone better. Take your time, get to know the next boy—man—before you get too involved. There's someone out there for everyone.'

'Lots of someones for some people,' she added in an undertone, but not so quietly Nick missed it. Was she talking about him or her father? Nick had no idea, but he suspected that in Annabelle's mind he and her father were about on a par as far as reliability with women was concerned.

Melody, however, wasn't going to be soothed any time soon, and she continued to alternate between tears and anger all the way to town.

'Okay,' Annabelle said to her when Nick stopped the car outside the house. 'This is where we live. I've been up all night with you, and Nick's missed a great bush breakfast. He and I are both hungry and I'm tired and cranky as well. You can use the phone to call your father, you can have first shower, I'll even see if I can find some clothes to fit you, though it will probably have to be a tracksuit, but, please, just while we get ourselves sorted, stop talking about killing people.'

Melody looked at her in surprise then said, 'It's not *my* fault Jack hurt me.'

With that she climbed out of the car and marched towards the house, Annabelle's caustic 'No?' floating behind her.

## CHAPTER EIGHT

ANNABELLE was not so hard-hearted that Melody's plight didn't touch her, but the young woman's self-obsessed attitude made feeling too much sympathy impossible. After providing her with clean clothes and toiletries—the hospital had a supply of toothbrushes—and leaving her in the bathroom, Annabelle headed for the kitchen, determined to have a really good Sunday breakfast of bacon and eggs, even hash browns if they had some potatoes.

But as she crossed the living room she sniffed the air.

Bacon sizzling somewhere.

She found Nick out at the barbeque, the bacon spitting as it crisped, eggs and tomato slices lined up beside him.

'Toast as well?' he asked, pointing to where he had the toaster plugged in at an outside power point.

'The lot!' Annabelle declared, and could have hugged him, for if there was one thing she needed after a sleepless night, it was a decent breakfast.

Hugging him was, of course, out of the question. For her at least, although not long after that, while Annabelle

made toast, Melody appeared, looking far more glamor-
ous in Annabelle's tracksuit than she ever had.

'Oh, breakfast, you wonderful man,' Melody declared,
flinging her arms around the cook and holding him for
far too long.

Maybe I'll burn just one piece of toast—Melody's—
Annabelle thought then dismissed the meanness as being
overtiredness. In fact, she gave the very nicest piece
of toast to their guest, and as they all settled around
the table, she even kept her mouth shut while Melody
warbled on about Daddy's plane and Daddy's boat and
their holiday villa in the south of France.

'We're going there next week and will be there for two
months. If you have any time off, you'd be welcome.'

The invitation was directed at Nick, who turned it
aside by offering more toast.

'Jetting off to the south of France in the next couple of
months? Didn't you say you were on leave?' Annabelle
asked Nick as they washed and dried the breakfast
dishes while Melody remained outside to phone Daddy
and arrange a lift home.

'I'm *here* for the next couple of months,' Nick reminded her, but something in the way he spoke made her
look more closely at him. He was staring out the window,
his hand swirling the dishmop around an already clean
plate—definitely distracted.

By a barely adult blonde on the phone, or by something else?

Annabelle dismissed the blonde idea—he'd shown
not the slightest interest in Melody for all she'd been
throwing herself at him—so what was bothering him?

The two-month placement?

Was he regretting it?

She thought back to the conversation at dinner the previous evening, when Grandfather Cartwright had talked about the town needing a doctor. Something then had triggered that slight frown between Nick's eyebrows...

Annabelle reined in her thoughts as she realised that if she hadn't been watching Nick so closely—giving the impression of being a love-sick adolescent like Melody—she wouldn't have noticed frowns or slight differences of tone in conversations. When had she started this focus on her colleague? And why?

That last question she didn't want to answer—far easier to go with when. She'd, naturally enough, been shocked by his revelations about his wife's abortion and she'd felt his hurt. Watching over him after that had only been the natural sympathy of a colleague.

A nasty swirling in her stomach told her that was a lie and all the warnings she'd given Melody about getting to know a man before getting too involved reverberated in her head. Not that she was getting involved—they'd sorted that out earlier.

'I can stay here with Melody until she's rescued, if you want to go out and visit your father.'

Nick's suggestion made the swirling in her stomach tighten into a knot, while a chill swept through her.

She *should* go, she *had* to go—it was why she'd taken this placement—but was she ready?

Of course she was.

'I don't think so,' she told Nick, telling herself it wasn't right to leave the pair of them alone—protecting Nick, of course—but, in truth, since she'd realised her feelings for Nick were more than just sexual, she'd had to rethink her assumptions about her father—and consider her genetic inheritance.

Maybe Dad had fallen in love with the wrong women, women who were wrong for him—as she seemed to be doing with the wrong men, although two was hardly a workable sample.

'I need a good sleep,' she added when she realised Nick was waiting for more from her. 'I'll go next week.'

And she did need a sleep but, sleeping, could she prove an adequate chaperone?

And was she being stupid in this 'protecting Nick' thing? How likely was it that Melody would want to accuse him of impropriety some time in the future?

Well, given that that young woman was already plotting terrible revenge on the unfortunate Jack, it wasn't totally unlikely.

Headlines containing accusations of such behaviour from doctors and teachers flashed through Annabelle's head. Some people, men and women, had been guilty, but others had been falsely accused and it was part of ongoing training in her field to ensure such accusations couldn't be made against colleagues.

She'd sleep tonight.

Eileen's arrival, within minutes of this decision, changed everything.

'Betsy-Ann's phoned. There's been an accident.' Eileen put her arm around Annabelle's shoulder before she added, 'It's bad, love. She's called the flying doctor but you'd get there first.'

For a moment Annabelle's mind went completely blank, then her thoughts raced through all the denials, as adolescent a reaction as Melody's had been the night before.

*It can't be too bad! I haven't seen him! I haven't
made my peace!*

It was only by a supreme effort of will she didn't
stamp her foot. Then Nick had his arm around her where
Eileen's had been.

'Come on, I'll drive you out there. Eileen will take
care of Melody.'

Totally numb, Annabelle allowed herself to be led to
the troopie, protesting only when Nick opened the door,
delaying their departure long enough to call Bruce and
let him jump into the front seat to sit between them. The
journey would take an hour and if she had something
warm and alive to hold onto during it, she might just
survive it.

She gave directions when necessary, following a road
and then a track she knew so well but hadn't seen for
more than ten years. This wasn't how she should have
come home, this wasn't how things were meant to be, but
the closer they got to the mine and her father's camp, the
stronger the memories of all the good times became.

'We had trail bikes, Kitty and I, handed down from
the older girls, and we rode them far further than Dad
would have known. This was our kingdom, and one
day a handsome prince would seek us here, not hacking
through years of vines and jungle, as Sleeping Beauty's
prince had had to do, but crossing this almost trackless
land to find us.'

Nick listened to her reminiscences, finding comfort
in the fact her voice was growing stronger. But as he
drove he wondered what it must have been like for a
young girl growing up in such isolation. Had the women
she'd said had come and gone in her father's life cared
for his daughters? Something Eileen had said suggested

Annabelle had brought up not only herself but her sister as well.

And just when had the woman beside him slipped beneath his skin so now he hurt for her and was filled with frustration that he couldn't take away her pain?

'That's it, up ahead,' Annabelle said, her voice hoarse again with unshed tears.

Nick looked into the distance, seeing a big hill, or small mountain, carved practically in two.

'Sometimes you literally have to move mountains to find good opal,' Annabelle said. 'First you blast away the top and shift all the overburden, then you dig, often down another twenty or thirty feet before you come across a seam. Sometimes you never come across a good seam. I suppose it's a bit like love—you need some luck.'

There was nothing to be said to that remark, so Nick drove on, seeing that there was a platform of earth about halfway down the hill and a road winding down from it. Closer now, he could see a collection of corrugated-iron buildings, one main one and several smaller ones, like shiny silver chickens clustered around their silver mother hen.

'Generator shed, equipment shed, cutting shed and main quarters—there are two caravans under the roof of the big shed that act as bedrooms for guests.'

Nick guessed it was easier for her to talk about the physical details of what lay ahead of them than think of the emotional hurdle she was going to have to leap if her father's accident proved fatal.

'Follow the track up the slope,' Annabelle told him, and Nick made out the shape and colour of a big four-wheel-drive police vehicle on the flattened area halfway up the mountain. There was also what appeared to be a bulldozer manoeuvring around up there.

Nick pulled up beside the police car and was about to go round to open Annabelle's door when he realised she was already halfway across the ground between where they'd parked and a large hole in the ground.

'Don't go any closer.'

A man's voice shouted the order and as Nick hurried forward, the big first-aid chest in his arms, he saw a policeman catch Annabelle in his arms.

He was still holding her, talking soothingly, when Nick joined them, dropping the chest and looking enquiringly at the man.

'Seems he was on a good seam. Betsy-Ann says he was, and he must have forgotten everything else, including basic safety. Apparently he got down off the excavator to check a piece he'd pulled out of the seam, and the ground holding the excavator collapsed, the bucket hitting him.'

'But he always got down to check the rocks he pulled out,' Annabelle protested, 'and he knew the dangers. He was *always* careful, making sure the bucket of the excavator was on the ground beyond the hole.'

'Let's not argue hows,' Nick said gently. 'If he's still alive, we need to get to him.'

The policeman introduced himself as Neil and pointed to the bulldozer. 'My young constable is a farm boy so he can drive those things. He's just hooked up a chain to the excavator and is backing off enough to hold the weight of the machine so anyone who goes down there doesn't become another casualty.'

A signal from the constable told him he had the excavator stable, and telling Annabelle to stay right where she was Nick headed for the hole.

'He's always careful,' a shaky voice behind him said, and he sighed. He should have known she'd disobey him, and it *was* her father.

'See,' Annabelle continued, 'first you excavate enough to make a shelf for the machine to sit on while you dig deeper. Dad *always* checked the shelf was solid.'

They were scrambling down onto the shelf as she spoke, close to the huge excavator that lay tilted to one side like an enormous, injured beast. The bucket on the end of its long extended arm might have been on the ground beyond the hole when Mr Donne climbed down, but the way the machine tilted had dropped it into the lowest part, where the trapped body of a man was now visible.

'Annabelle, you don't want to be here—you have my promise I'll do everything I can to save him.'

Nick may as well have spoken to the walls for all the notice Annabelle took. In fact, now she moved ahead of him, nimbly scrambling from one rock to the next, finally arriving beside her father.

'He's alive,' she called to Nick, but as Nick took in the outward appearance of the accident he wondered just how badly wounded the man was. The heavy metal digging bucket had landed on his chest.

Annabelle was clawing at the dirt beneath her father, desperate to release him from the trap, but Nick knew that releasing him might also release blood from badly damaged major blood vessels now sealed off by the weight of the bucket.

He examined the man as well as he could. Thready pulse, his skin cold and clammy, unconscious at the moment, though his free hand moved as Annabelle kept talking to him—talking while she dug.

They *had* to get him out. Even knowing the risk, there was really no alternative. Nick turned to the two policemen who had followed them down.

'Do you think between us we can lift the bucket off him? The machine is tilted to the right so if we move the bucket that way, we shouldn't compromise the stability.'

'Don't move it!'

The voice was weak but the words were unmistakeable.

'Dad!' Annabelle shrieked, holding hard to her father's hand.

'I knew you'd come home, Annabelle,' he said, each word coming out so slowly Nick knew what an effort it was for the man to speak. Crushed ribs, probably deflated lungs, no air to form the words.

'Of course I did, Dad,' Annabelle told him. 'I'm just sorry it took so long—sorry I was so stubborn.'

'Love you, kid,' the man said, and Nick had to swallow hard as Gerald Donne's eyes closed and his pulse grew even weaker.

'We've got to try to save him,' Nick said. Determination to save Annabelle any more pain lent conviction to his words. 'Annabelle, you come around this side—there'll be bleeding when we move the bucket, you'll have to do your best to stem it.'

Neil took over the physical placements of the three of them who would lift the bucket and when they were where he wanted them he gave the order to lift and move it.

Nick was so busy making sure no one else was injured

in this manoeuvre he couldn't keep an eye on the patient, but Annabelle's cry of despair told him he'd guessed right.

Once the bucket was clear, he returned to his patient and saw that the man's chest had somehow been torn open, pulsing blood telling him there was at least one torn artery.

'It's more important to stop the loss of blood than worry about spinal complications and we can't work on him here, so let's carry him up closer to the car and the medical chest.'

The policemen were obviously as aware of the urgency of the situation as Annabelle and Nick were, so Gerald was carried quickly out of the hole, the three men carrying while Annabelle pressed an increasingly bloody pad on her father's chest.

Working more swiftly than he'd ever worked in his medical life, Nick found the tear and sutured the ruptured aorta, the main source of blood loss, but blood still flowing from lower in the chest told him there were more problems. The main vein returning blood to the heart, the vena cava, must also be torn. Finding this tear was more difficult as the damaged ribs and lungs prevented him getting a clear view of it.

Annabelle had fitted a mask over her father's mouth and nose and was using a hand-held respirator bag to push oxygen into his lungs.

'He's going to die, isn't he?' she whispered.

'Not if I can help it,' Nick snapped. 'Now, get your nurse's head on and keep it on. Neil, you take over the bag from Annabelle. Annabelle, you start cleaning out this mess, flush with saline, see if you can see a thick vein we can follow up or down to where the tear is.'

Nick was picking pieces of shattered bone out of the open chest wound, hoping to release some of the pressure on the lungs, determined to save this man, the father of the woman he loved.

Loved?

Where had that come from?

He barely knew her, had known her only a week—

'And *you* get your doctor head on!'

Startled looks from both Annabelle and Neil told him he'd spoken this order to himself out loud.

'I often talk to myself,' he said by way of explanation, although that wasn't true at all. It had only been the last few days that he'd found himself doing it more and more. Usually telling himself to stop thinking about his colleague.

'Plane's here! I'll go down and bring the crew up.'

The young constable spoke as the shadow of the flying doctor's plane passed over the scene of desperation on the ground.

Nick said a silent prayer of thanks but kept working, knowing time was getting short.

A sudden twitch, an easing of the blood flow, a cry from Annabelle, and Nick knew they'd lost their patient. Without hesitation he thrust his hand into the man's shattered chest, felt for the shape of his heart and began squeezing rhythmically, pumping what blood he could around the man's body. He knew it was still leaking out, but if he could keep it flowing to the brain—

'Okay, mate.' The new voice was gentle but authoritative, and the hand on his shoulder was firm. 'You did your best but sometimes we have to say enough.'

Nick looked up at Annabelle, squatting opposite him, one hand holding tightly to her father's.

She nodded.

'It's best he goes here, in the place he loved,' she whispered. 'But thank you, Nick, for trying.'

Nick stood up and held out his hand to the man who'd spoken to him, then realised how it looked and took it back. It was the same doctor who had come out to Jane Crenshaw but a different nurse.

'How about you go down to the camp and get cleaned up?' Neil suggested. 'Take Annabelle with you.'

Nick had found a cloth in the first-aid kit and was wiping his hands and shirt as best he could. He looked at Annabelle, who shook her head.

'I think we'll stay here,' he said, but he moved towards her, put his arm around her shoulders and led her away so her father's body could be loaded onto a stretcher.

'There's an ambulance on the way from Murrawingi,' Neil told them. 'There'll have to be an autopsy so we'll take him there. You know Betsy-Ann's down at the camp. Do you want to tell her or should I?'

He was speaking to Annabelle but Nick answered.

'Best if you do it,' he said. 'I'll take care of Annabelle.'

Annabelle heard the words through the thick fog of grief and disbelief that had enveloped her and she wished with all her heart they had more than a professional meaning. Not since her father had failed her had she ever expected or even wanted a man to take care of her—not even Graham—so why was she thinking this way?

Because, for all her warnings to herself, the man they called Storm had slipped beneath her defences?

Rubbish!

She shivered and Nick's arm tightened around her

shoulders. All willpower gone, she leant into him, drawing his warmth into her cold body, drawing comfort into her aching heart.

'Oh, Nick,' she whispered, and he must have heard the anguish in her voice because he took her in his arms and held her close while she let the tears she'd been holding back flow freely. And when the tears stopped she took his hand and led him to the edge of the manmade plateau, settling on a boulder there and looking out over the camp and the wide-stretching plains beneath them.

'This is what I love,' she told him, her voice still rusty with her tears. 'This view. It was so much part of me that I cried every night for a year when our mother took Kitty and me away from Dad. Every day I'd bring his smoko up, and we'd sit here, Kitty, me and him, and we'd talk about the land and how it was formed and how the opal got its colour and the magic of it all. The first day I cooked scones—they were appalling—Dad was so full of praise for them I thought I'd burst.'

Nick understood the magic part—the land out here was weaving a spell over him already—but the rest? The scones?

'Your mother wasn't here all the time?'

Annabelle looked surprised.

'I thought I'd told you that—about Dad and his women. Mum left when I was seven, Kitty was only three, and though women came and went, there were often times when it was just the three of us, Kitty, Dad and me. Then, two days before my fourteenth birthday, who should turn up but Mum? With a court order giving her custody of the two of us.'

Nick heard the deep intake of breath and realised his companion was fighting off more tears.

'I thought Dad would refuse. I mean, Kitty didn't even remember Mum, but he said we had to go and that it was for the best and so we went and then he would sometimes write or send us cards if he was in town, but—'

She choked on the last word and Nick didn't press her. It was bad enough a father had betrayed his daughter's love by letting her go off with a mother who'd already deserted her once.

He held the grieving woman close and let her cry again, knowing tears would help the healing, wondering why men didn't realise that and use the release more readily.

'I'm okay,' she said at last, moving away from him. 'I'd better see if there's anything I can do down at the camp, although, knowing Betsy-Ann, she's already got dibs on anything of any value and will be organising everything without too much consultation with anyone.'

Nick smiled to himself, although there was little joy in the situation, but there'd been no bitterness in Annabelle's voice as she'd spoken of her half-sister and he realised she was over whatever bitchiness she'd felt earlier. She was stating a fact—this sister was obviously the organiser and if she organised things to her own advantage, Annabelle didn't really care.

But she didn't move far away, halting, apparently, as another chilling thought struck her.

'I'll have to tell Kitty—or Joe, her boyfriend, and let him tell her. She hasn't seen Dad since she was ten and we hadn't heard from him the last six years so I don't think she'll be...'

Annabelle's voice broke and Nick finished the sentence for her.

'As devastated as you are?' he said, holding her close again.

'We were such mates,' she whispered. 'That's why I couldn't understand it all. First him letting us go like that, then not helping out a few years later when Mum went off with some new bloke she'd met up with. When I first wrote to tell him we were on our own, he wrote back and said come home, and I'd have come straight back here, although I'd already started university, but I knew Kitty was really clever. She was doing so well at school and was already determined to be a doctor. School of the Air is good, but not for high school when you need to get top marks in the final year and especially as we didn't have computer access out here. I wrote to Dad, explaining this and asking if he could help with some money. I'd found out we could get an allowance from the government but it wasn't enough to live on and pay rent. He never answered that letter, not a word, upset, I suppose, that we *didn't* go home.'

Nick's gut clenched at the enormity of this double betrayal. How could a man do that to his daughters? To any child?

'And what did you do?' he asked, trying to imagine the two young women—girls really—fending for themselves.

'I deferred my training for a year and worked full time and saved some money so we had something behind us, and Kitty took my part-time job and we managed. People do. And I suppose I can understand his attitude— he'd take care of us if we came home. That must have been his thinking. He probably thought we would eventually, but I couldn't do that to Kitty.'

They sat a little longer, Bruce returning from an

exciting chase after a kangaroo who'd had little to fear from him. He panted to a stop in front of them, tongue lolling and looking exceedingly pleased with himself. Annabelle reached out and patted him.

'Good dog,' she said, then she put her arms around him and gave him a hug.

Distancing herself from her human companion? Nick wondered. Embarrassed she'd wept in his arms?

He suspected she was, and knew he was right when she stood up and said, 'If you don't mind, I'll walk back to the camp.'

He hated leaving her, hurting as she was, and had to physically force himself to walk back to the car, every step dragging heavily. It was because she was so alone, the bits and pieces that he knew of her life revealing that she'd been this way for a long time. Oh, she'd had her sister—still did—and they were obviously close. Annabelle had taken the responsibility for her sister on her shoulders but who'd been there for Annabelle? First deserted by her father, then by her mother, then a plea for help ignored…

Nick drove back to the camp, anger he didn't entirely understand burning inside him, so when Betsy-Ann, having introduced herself and asked where Annabelle was, remarked that of course her sister wouldn't help her sort out the mess in their father's office, Nick wanted to belt her one.

He didn't, offering to help instead.

'You'd better get cleaned up first,' Betsy-Ann said, and he realised he was covered in blood and dirt.

'This way,' the woman said, leading him out the door and around the side of the shed to where four pieces of corrugated iron had been attached to the props of a tall tank-stand.

'I'll see if Dad's got any decent gear you can have,' she said, showing no emotion, even though the blood all over his clothes was her father's.

She returned only minutes later with a very faded chambray shirt and a pair of shorts that might have seen better days but were clean and pressed. And if putting on a dead man's clothes might have been offputting, the fact that they'd belonged to Annabelle's father somehow made it all right.

Which was another weird idea he'd have to consider later—like the love one that had popped into his head.

Once back inside, he offered his help once again.

'You could try moving that filing cabinet,' Betsy-Ann suggested immediately. 'I can see all kinds of papers down behind it but although I've got most of the stuff out of the drawers, I can't budge it.'

Nick checked the metal filing cabinet, tugging at it experimentally then finally tipping it forward. It dug into the earthen floor of the shed and he realised that was why it wouldn't slide out from the wall, having embedded itself into the dirt.

'If I tip it further forward, can you reach in and pull the papers out?' he asked.

Betsy-Ann decided she could do that and together they managed to salvage a pile of envelopes and invoices and heaven only knew what else.

'I'll leave them all on this desk and you can sort it,' she said to Nick. 'I'm putting anything with Annabelle or Kitty's name on it in that box there, and all the other stuff into this larger box. I'm not staying out here on my own so I'll take it home and sort it there. Neil wants to look at something in the cutting shed and I want to check what he's doing. Dad's best opal is in there.'

Having been given his orders, Nick poked a finger into the dusty, cobwebby pile of paper on the desk. This was stuff that had obviously fallen down behind the filing cabinet, possibly over the last ten years, but if it would save Annabelle the pain of seeing her father's writing, he'd sort through it.

He obediently checked each paper, throwing invoices and bills, anything about the business, into the big box, while a few notes and letters with Annabelle's or Kitty's names on them, some old photos he'd like to look at later, and paintings the two had apparently done as children, all went into Annabelle's box. One letter, the ink faded but with a neat sender's address on the back—Annabelle Donne and a Brisbane address—looked unopened but old envelopes often stuck themselves back down. He threw it into the box with the other things and had just found an old rag to wipe the dust off the desk when Annabelle walked in.

# CHAPTER NINE

'THE ambulance has just left. Can we go?' she said, and when Nick nodded she walked out again, heading directly to the troopie, not bothering with farewells to either her sister or the policeman. Nick picked up the box and followed her. He wasn't sure if this was all of Annabelle and Kitty's stuff or even if he was meant to take it, but he had a feeling that it would a be a long time before Annabelle came out here again, so she should have the things, even if she didn't want to go through them just yet.

He put the box in the back of the troopie, allowed Bruce to sit in front again, and hesitated before starting the engine.

'Yes, of course I should say goodbye to them but I just can't,' Annabelle muttered to him, moving something wrapped in an old rag off the seat and setting it on the floor before sitting down herself.

Nick could see she was close to breaking down again, so he didn't argue, simply started the car and drove off, waving as two figures appeared at the door of one of the sheds.

They drove home in silence, apart from Annabelle directing him to turn left or right when they came to

junctions in the road. Used now to the dry water channels running through the country, Nick eased the vehicle
in and out of them, not wanting to jolt his passenger too
much.

The best news of the day—not that it had much to
beat—was that Eileen had apparently whisked Melody
away—or perhaps her father's plane had already collected her—but for whatever reason the house was
empty, and strangely welcoming, as if it had already
become a home...

Aware she had to drag herself out of the cloud of
emptiness enveloping her but unable to find an exit from
it, Annabelle grabbed her rag-wrapped bundle, walked
in and sank down on the lounge.

'How about I phone your sister or her boyfriend?'
Nick offered, and Annabelle looked up at him, even
through the cloud registering the concern on his face.

She shook her head, sighed and said, 'There's a
small tartan notebook on the desk in my bedroom. Joe's
number is in there under Kitty, and their mobile numbers, they could be anywhere.'

Nick collected the notebook and brought it and his
mobile back to the lounge where he sat down next to
Annabelle.

'I'll get the number then you can decide if you want
to talk. Either way I'll be here to take over if you want
me to, and I'll hold you while you do it.'

Annabelle wanted so desperately to thank him, but
even more she wanted to refuse the offer he was making—to handle this herself. She'd handled things before
so why was she falling apart now and letting this man
prop her up?

'I hate this,' she said, and saw him try to hide a smile.

'Relying on someone else, you mean?' he teased, but so gently she felt the tears dripping down her cheeks once again. She knew her eyes would be red, her face all splotchy, and suddenly she hated it that Nick was seeing her like this—hated it even more than being so reliant on him.

'Pathetic,' she muttered, more to herself than to him. 'That's what I am. Go on, get the number, but I'll talk.'

She got as far as 'Dad's dead' before she knew she couldn't handle it, and passed the phone to Nick before heading into her bedroom, throwing herself on the bed and curling into a tight ball, as if being as small as possible might help ease the pain that racked her body.

Nick explained what had happened to the extremely sensible young woman on the other end of the phone, who explained her lack of deep emotion by saying, 'I never really knew him that well, but Annabelle, she adored him. She's going to be devastated. Do you think I should come out?'

'Could you?' Nick asked, and heard a sigh.

'I've got exams at the moment but I could probably get a couple of them deferred, though if she knew I'd done that she'd kill me and then she'd have no one.'

Nick smiled to himself, thinking how well this young woman knew her sister.

'She said on the phone the other day that Eileen's there,' Kitty continued, 'and you—are you kind of friendly enough with her to give her some support? I know she's scratchy as all get-out around men these days, thanks to ratfink Graham, but if you could kind of be supportive...'

'I can do supportive,' Nick assured Kitty, then heard soft snuffling noises and knew she'd started to weep, not as inured to her father's death as she'd made out.

'Have *you* got someone with you?' he asked.

A muffled 'Joe's here. I'll be fine' reassured Nick, although Kitty didn't sound all that fine. When Joe, however, took the phone, Nick was satisfied. Joe sounded eminently sensible, even offering to bring Kitty out if Nick thought it necessary.

'I'll keep in touch and let you know if it is,' Nick promised, 'and I'll make sure Annabelle phones Kitty when she's up to it.'

After more assurances and counter-assurances he ended the call and cautiously entered Annabelle's bedroom.

She was curled in a foetal position in the middle of the big bed, eyes open, staring blankly into space.

'Get you anything?' he asked quietly.

She shook her head and then he saw that the tears he'd thought had dried up were still spilling from her eyes and he crossed to the bed and lifted her so he could hold her in his arms. Humans weren't made to be alone in their sorrow—he knew that from his work, knew the comfort of a fellow human's arms could at least help ease the pain.

When the comfort turned to something else he didn't know, but at some stage the gentle kisses he'd been pressing on the top of her head as he'd prompted her to remember happy things about her father slid down onto the skin at her temple, and as her head turned slightly, their lips met.

Grief wore many guises, Nick knew, but as Annabelle's body pressed against his, and their kisses became more fervent, he also knew he had to draw away.

'Please, Nick,' she whispered, hands clinging to his shoulders. 'It's only for oblivion, that's all. And only for today.'

He saw her chest rise as she drew in a deep breath, looked up at him and tried a smile.

'I know I'm red-eyed and splotchy and not exactly your type, but your body wants this as much as mine does.'

Another deep breath lifted her chest, and she continued, her voice a husky whisper. 'I might have been naive when I fell for Graham but I'm not so stupid I'd mistake comfort for love so you have no fear that I'd want more than comfort from you. I know the last thing you want is commitment of any kind, and given my genetic inheritance it's probably impossible for me, no matter how much I might wish for it, but for now, Nick?'

He wanted her so badly his whole body ached. He closed his eyes and pictured himself feasting on her breasts, probing the slick warmth of her inner body, tasting all of her as she learnt and tasted him. He gathered her close, he even kissed her again, on the lips, but chastely now, the heat of minutes earlier held in check by only the most iron-hard control.

She'd understood it wasn't going to happen and eased away, looking into his face, trying hard to smile.

'You're thinking I'd hate you in the morning?' she said, her voice gravelly with tears and probably desire, but making light of the situation as best she could.

He kissed her again.

'I think you might hate *yourself* in the morning,' he said gently.

Hate herself in the morning? She hated herself now! She'd all but begged the man to make love to her and he'd rejected her. Not that rejection was new, but they had to continue to live together for seven more weeks...

Lost in her own confusion, she didn't realise Nick was still talking.

'But I wasn't thinking that,' she heard him say.

'No?'

'No,' he murmured, and dropped the lightest of kisses on the frown between her eyebrows. 'I was thinking what if it's not comfort?'

He couldn't believe he'd said it—and obviously she couldn't believe it either for she continued frowning at him, finally standing up off the bed, shaking her head and saying, 'Oh, Nick, if only...' before walking out of the room.

*If only*? The words repeated themselves in his head and as he heard the shower turned on in the bathroom he wondered just how she might have finished them.

If only she could trust him?

If only she could believe him?

If only she could love him back?

He sighed, realising that belief and trust were different sides of the same coin, and neither of them would come easily to her, given the betrayal she'd suffered both from her father and her lover.

As for love, how could he even consider she might love him? Knowing what she did of his failure in the relationship stakes, he'd be the last person on earth with whom she'd want to get involved.

Annabelle made it to the bathroom without crying

again, but once she was under the blessed force of the hot bore water, crying didn't matter, because the tears just added to the general wetness.

What if it wasn't comfort? he'd said.

What if—?

Was her 'if only' reply a dead giveaway of how *she* felt?

What if? he'd said.

Two little words but, oh, how much they hurt.

It was stupid to be thinking the 'what if it wasn't comfort?' meant he loved her. This was Nick Tempest, the man who'd been there and done that as far as love and commitment were concerned, and she was a woman who needed both.

Besides, how likely was it that Nick Tempest, who could have virtually any single woman in the hospital, would fall in love with her?

They barely knew each other.

But *you* love *him*, some small voice in her head piped up.

That's different, she told it. He's been understanding and kind and he's a great doctor so it's not so surprising I would—well, not fall in love but kind of learn to love the man...

Determined to pull herself together, she turned off the shower, dried herself hastily, then, praying Nick had left her bedroom, scuttled in that direction, unable to not notice him sitting on the lounge, a cardboard carton beside him.

Had he had some things sent out to him?

He didn't appear to be searching through the contents, just sitting there, the box beside him.

Deciding she was done with tears—for the moment

anyway—and that hiding in the bedroom didn't help her grief—or her confusion over Nick's *what if* remark—she dressed and went to join him.

'I'm okay now,' she announced. 'I guess I had to get rid of a certain volume of tears and hopefully that's done. I'll mourn Dad in my heart for a long time, but I won't cry all over you any more.'

He smiled at her, the kind of Nick-smile that ripped something loose in her chest so her heart did a little jitterbug before settling, more or less, back into normal rhythm.

'That would be a pity when I've promised Kitty and Joe I'll support you, and if offering a chest to cry on isn't support, then I don't know what is.'

How pathetic was *she*? A smile and a few kind words and one of those stupid cry lumps had settled in her throat.

Again!

She swallowed hard then nodded at the box.

'Ah, the box,' he said. 'Apparently it's stuff of yours and Kitty's. Betsy-Ann was sorting through things in your dad's office, putting anything with your names on it into this box. I brought it back from the camp. Will we go through it?'

Annabelle heard the words but her mind didn't register them. She was trying to work out the timeframe. Had her half-sister been going through their father's papers before he'd even died?

And if so, did it really matter?

She told herself it was probably just Betsy-Ann's way of coping and turned her attention back to Nick.

'What kind of things?'

Before Nick could reply, the phone interrupted them.

For a whole five seconds he considered ignoring it but training and professionalism wouldn't allow that, even if it turned out to be nothing more than a social call.

Not social at all—the elderly Mrs Warren was on the other end, all but hysterical.

The lump in Oscar's neck, she wailed at Nick, had grown so much he couldn't eat, couldn't swallow, not even water.

Nick looked at Annabelle, who couldn't have helped but hear the conversation, and saw her looking alive and alert once again.

'Don't even think about it,' he said to her, holding his hand over the phone so Mrs Warren wouldn't hear the argument he knew was about to take place.

'But you phoned your friend and you looked it up on the internet—it's most likely a benign fibroma. Are you just going to let Oscar starve to death or die from dehydration? Come on, Nick, don't you see it's just what I need to take my mind off Dad for a while? An operation on a dog! What could make a better diversion?'

He'd already knocked back the other diversion she'd suggested so he found himself telling Mrs Warren to bring Oscar up to the hospital.

'I'm not operating on him in the operating theatre!' he warned Annabelle, hoping she'd hear the firmness in his voice and refrain from arguing.

She did. In fact, it seemed she was way ahead of him.

'There's an old stainless-steel table in that shed out the back that has all the junk on it. I'll drag it out and cover it with thick plastic. We can use the back veranda because we can hose it down, although I can spread plastic under the table as well—'

Nick held up his hand. He knew she'd seized on arranging the entire operation to block out her sorrow, but he should have some say in what was going on!

'You go into Theatre and sort some instruments, gloves, basic antiseptic, sutures, swabs etcetera. I'll get the table and organise the plastic, then find the drugs we'll need to knock him out.'

He was pleased to win a smile from her, small though it was.

'Thank you, Nick,' she said, and he felt she wasn't thanking him for agreeing to undertake the operation on a dog of all things, but thanking him for his support.

And quite possibly for not making love to her when she'd all but begged for it.

His body was still telling him how foolish *that* decision had been, but he knew it had been the right one, although as he watched her head across to the hospital, her shoulders straightening as she detached herself, if only temporarily, from her grief, he knew his body wasn't going to get over wanting her any time soon.

Why?

She was nothing like the women he usually sought for company—far too challenging for a start.

It was the slipping-beneath-his-skin thing…

A vehicle pulling up outside the hospital reminded him this was not the time for thinking about the mystery that was his attraction to Annabelle. In fact, there probably was no good time, so he should accept it was nothing more than proximity and stop thinking about it at all.

Like that was possible!

He headed for the shed where it seemed decades of old hospital equipment had been stored. Was there some rule about not disposing of government supplies permanently?

By the time he had the table set up, thick plastic from the storeroom unrolled beneath it, and more across the top, Annabelle had wheeled a trolley, with instruments, swabs and dressings neatly laid out on it, onto the veranda.

Nick found a short-acting anaesthetic, guessed at the dog's approximate weight, using his old Labrador as a comparison, and prepared a syringe. He attached a new paper mask to a tube, the tube to a small oxygen tank, and carried those out as well.

'I'll hold his paw,' Mrs Warren announced, and one look at her wrinkled face was enough to warn Nick not to argue.

'There'll be blood,' he warned her.

'Fiddlesticks,' she snapped. 'As if a bit of blood'd bother me. Didn't I kill my own chickens from the day I married Mr Warren? I've got a sheep hanging in the meat safe, he said to me when we got out to the house after the wedding, but it'll need a day or two, so grab a chicken and we'll have that for tea. Grab a chicken, I said to him, and do what? Wring its neck, let it bleed then pluck it, woman. I nearly left him there and then, but love finds a way, doesn't it?'

Nick looked across at his surgical assistant to see how she'd taken these revelations and found she was smiling.

'Perhaps it does,' she said to Mrs Warren, as Nick slid the anaesthetic into Oscar and together they watched it work.

Uncertain whether the timing of the anaesthetic's effects would be the same for a dog as for a human, Nick then settled Oscar into a position where he could get at the fibroma, and taped the dog's paws—except for the one Mrs Warren held—to the table.

'I found this!' Annabelle announced, holding up what looked like an old cut-throat razor. 'I thought it would be better than a scalpel to shave his hair away.'

So wielding a razor his great-grandfather had probably thought old-fashioned, Nick shaved the hair on Oscar's neck, giving him a clean area of skin to make a cut. Annabelle swabbed the area carefully, and Nick began, repeating in his head the instructions he'd read on the internet.

'Could it be cancer?' Mrs Warren asked.

'It could,' Nick told her, 'but it's unlikely. From what I can find out, it's just a lump of tissue, sometimes formed around an old injury, and sometimes inexplicable, but I'll send the lump to a vet friend of mine and get it tested so we know for sure.'

Mrs Warren seemed satisfied with that, and totally unfazed by blood as she moved closer to peer into the incision Nick had made.

Uncertain of the anatomy of dogs, he took his time separating out the small blood vessels, tying off any bleeders, making sure he didn't cut a tendon or, worse, the dog's oesophagus or trachea. As he moved the lump with his gloved fingers, he saw it was bigger than it had seemed and understood why Oscar had been having difficulty swallowing.

'It's not attached to the oesophagus or growing out of it, is it?' Annabelle asked, obviously seeing what he'd just discovered.

'No, it's loose, just close to the oesophagus, and some

of the surrounding tissue is connected to oesophageal tissue, but we can cut that away without any damage.'

We!

A tiny word but it brought so much warmth to Annabelle's grief-frozen body she almost smiled.

Almost!

She didn't want to think about her father's death, and knew it was selfish of her to be feeling so much regret at not visiting and talking to him before he'd died, but thinking about her behaviour earlier with Nick—well, she didn't need to wait for morning to feel embarrassed.

'Swab, girl,' Mrs Warren said sharply, and Annabelle brought one hundred per cent of her attention back to the job they were doing. Oscar deserved that. Nick deserved it as well. She thought he'd probably have operated on Oscar anyway, but knew he'd decided to do it now to divert *her* attention from her grief.

And it had worked to the extent that although that heavy weight of sadness remained wedged in her chest, she was thinking more clearly now—well, most of the time.

Having removed the lump, Nick was now tidying up the tissues before stitching up the wound.

'Unfortunately, the hospital doesn't have those cone-shaped pieces of equipment vets use to keep dogs from licking their wounds and tearing the stitches out, but if you and Annabel stay here with Oscar, I'll see what I can do about a makeshift one.'

'He's a good man,' Mrs Warren said, nodding at Nick's departing figure.

Annabelle nodded her agreement, but Mrs Warren wasn't finished.

'Your dad was too. I was sorry to hear about his death. He was sick, you know, not with the women but with the obsession about the opal. He just forgot about the women when he was on some good colour and women don't like that—they couldn't cope with him ignoring them—that's why they left, but at heart he was a good man. He helped my Bob out one time. I've not forgotten that.'

Annabelle knew Mrs Warren's summing up was right, so it made her father ignoring her appeal even harder to understand. She should have written again, asked why he hadn't answered, but her own hurt pride had held her back. That and the fact she'd probably still been nurturing anger at him over his lack of fight when their mother had swept Kitty and her away.

Stupid pride—that's what it had been—and it had caused *her* more hurt than it had probably caused her father...

Nick returned before she could delve further into the whys and wherefores of the past, a cone-shaped object clutched triumphantly in his hand.

'I'll put it around then staple it together,' he said as he unwound a clear, thick plastic X-ray sheet to show how he'd achieved his success.

Oscar was stirring now, so Nick lifted him down onto the veranda, Mrs Warren holding him still until he was fully conscious. Nick attached the collar while Annabelle cleaned up, wrapping everything they'd used in the thick plastic.

Except for the cut-throat razor, which could be heat sterilised in the autoclave. It didn't look precious but it was a reminder of a bygone age, and as it had come in useful once in modern medicine, maybe it would again.

She was in the equipment room when Nick returned from carrying Oscar out to the car.

'Job well done?' he said, and she turned towards him, hearing the caution in his voice, knowing he wasn't certain just what kind of mood he'd find her in.

It came without warning. Oh, there'd been inklings of it, suspicious moments of awareness, but suddenly she knew that what she felt for this man—the one man in her orbit she should have most avoided—was love, a warm, overwhelming kind of love that filled her body, filtering into it like bulldust into crevices, even easing the heavy burden of her sadness slightly.

'Very well done,' she managed to reply, knowing that, above all, she had to hide any indication of that revelation from him. The pain love had already caused Nick had inoculated him against it. Love was the very last thing he wanted in his life for all his silly 'what if'...

And once again she felt a surge of gratitude that he'd resisted her pathetic pleas for love—no, for sex, for that was what she'd wanted at the time. The oblivion, if only for a moment, of sex...

'I suppose I should check with Eileen that Melody's okay,' she said, hoping that diversion would hide any indication of the wild thoughts tumbling through her head. They were ambling back to the house, and the house held beds, and she wasn't sure how strong her willpower was—

'I'll do it,' Nick told her, 'although reacquainting myself with Melody isn't high on my list of fun things to do. Was she for real? All that talk of Daddy and planes and the villa in France.'

The remark struck a wrong note in Annabelle's head. The life she'd assumed Nick led, while probably not including private planes and villas in France, was surely high-flying enough for these things not to seem to unusual?

Was her impression of his background wrong?

Did it matter?

After these two months, they'd have little to do with each other again—nothing, in fact, as she knew she couldn't work in his department the way she felt about him, and so she'd be moving to another hospital.

Again!

Perhaps she could stay out here, a permanent nurse, while the doctors could fly in for regular clinics. Everyone knew that once the drilling finished, the current arrangement would change...

# CHAPTER TEN

'MELODY'S gone, swept away in a helicopter by some-one local Daddy happened to know.' Nick returned as Annabelle was gloomily considering this future, al-though, to be honest, the idea of returning to a life out here would have delighted her not long ago, and still held a lot of promise. 'Do you want to look in the box?'

'What box?' she said, drawn out of her thoughts and totally bewildered, so for a moment she had no idea what he was talking about.

'The box I brought from your father's camp. I told you earlier. Betsy-Ann put anything with your or Kitty's names on it into a box. I brought it back for you.'

She was staring at him, her eyes wide with apprehen-sion, then she shrugged.

'What could there be of any interest?'

'You never know,' Nick told her, leading her towards the couch where the box she'd noticed earlier still sat.

Had things gone into it in order of age, or was it just coincidence that the first three things Annabelle pulled out were faded, splotchy 'artworks'—paintings she and Kitty must have done when they had been young, pos-sibly egged on by their teacher on School of the Air?

She smoothed them out with shaking fingers, so

touched that her father had kept them she couldn't speak, then she looked at the dust caked on her hands and held them up for Nick to inspect.

'Not so much treasured memories of his children as stuff that got stuck behind a cabinet or cupboard somewhere.'

'Now, you don't know that,' Nick chided her, pulling out a handkerchief and wiping her hands. 'Although,' he added as though prompted by honesty, 'there *were* a lot of things down behind the filing cabinet.'

But Annabelle was no longer listening, for she'd pulled out a parcel of envelopes, held together by a rubber band. They had her and Kitty's names written on the front of each, and the address they'd left when their mother had taken off. The top envelope was stamped 'Return to Sender'.

She frowned as she turned the letters over in her hand.

'I paid for mail to be forwarded for three months, and I told Dad our new address.' She was remembering out loud, wondering if her father *had* replied but the letter hadn't been forwarded. A date stamp—there had to be a date stamp. Letters posted here in town or in Murrawingi still had date stamps.

She peered at the faded lettering over the stamp, and sighed. January! Four months after they'd moved—one month after the mail-forwarding directions had run out.

But when she opened the envelope she could only shake her head in disbelief at the sheet of paper she found in it.

'He hated writing,' she said to Nick, aware tears were thickening her throat and choking her voice once again.

'He never had much schooling and found it difficult, but these are letters, Nick, letters he must have written when he stopped hearing from us. Perhaps because he was sorry about not helping out.'

She handed the sheet of paper, torn from a notebook, to Nick, knowing her eyes were too blurred to read the words.

'"Dear Annabelle and Kitty,"' Nick read out, '"I trust you are both well. I miss you both. Learn all you can so you can have good lives. Your loving father."'

Seeing the tears flowing freely again, Nick lifted the bundle of letters from Annabelle's hand.

'Perhaps now isn't the best time?' he said gently, but she shook her head.

'I need to hear them all. I need to know he cared. I *knew* he did, I knew that all along in my heart, but my stupid adolescent mind blamed him for everything—for Mum taking us first of all, then for not coming to our aid when she took off. So all my pain has been of my own making, but that's nothing to the pain I must have caused him.'

Nick's heart felt as if it was being torn in two by the torment in Annabelle's words, and he sat beside her and held her once again, taking out the second letter, not very different from the first, only adjuring the girls to be proud of themselves and to never let anyone look down on them.

'Good fatherly advice,' Nick said gently, as Annabelle took the letter and put it on top of the first, running her fingers over the words as if she could touch the hand of the man who'd written them.

There were four letters in all, perhaps written over a

period of years, for only the first one, the one stamped 'Return to Sender' had been posted.

'It doesn't make sense,' she said at last. 'There's no mention of the money at all. Even the first one doesn't mention my letter.'

Nick remembered the other letter he'd seen—the one he'd found in the mess of paper behind the filing cabinet. He dug through the box, ignoring old school exercise books and certificates showing how well either Kitty or Annabelle had performed in their school work. The letter had slipped down the side of the box to rest on the bottom, and he pulled it out and handed it to Annabelle.

'But that's my writing,' she pointed out. 'Far neater then than it is now.'

She turned it over in her hand, and ran her forefinger over the 'SWALK' printed in Biro on the seal at the back.

'How juvenile!' she muttered. 'I always wrote that on the back. Sealed with a loving kiss—boys probably don't do that.'

But Nick had stopped listening to her explanation. He took the letter out of her hand and peered more closely at the initials on the back.

'This letter hasn't been opened,' he said, pointing to where the neatly printed letters were still perfectly aligned. 'Maybe your father dropped the mail on top of the filing cabinet and it slipped behind it way back when he received it.'

'Way back when he received it.' She breathed the echo of his words then looked up at Nick, hardly daring to take the letter from his hands. 'Please tell me it's not *that* letter! Please tell me I haven't been estranged from my father for all these years because of a stupid mistake! A letter that wasn't ever read...'

Nick handed her the letter but she pushed it away.

'No, you read it,' she said, but she shook her head. 'Not that I don't know what it says. I *knew* Dad wouldn't just desert us, yet I let my stupid hurt pride and my anger at him keep us apart all those years. I blamed the fact he probably had a new woman and didn't have the money at the time, or the woman was looking after whatever money he made—that happened far too often—and wouldn't release any. There were so many feasible explanations I never for a moment thought he might not have got the letter or, having got it, not have read it.'

The letter was, indeed, Annabelle's plea for help, but couched in such apologetic terms Nick guessed the opal mine had never been a paying proposition. 'If you happen to be on a good seam,' Annabelle had written, further qualifying the request by assuring her father they'd manage somehow if he wasn't.

'Does opal ever pay?' he had to ask, and was pleased to see the question diverted her from her self-blaming thoughts.

'It pays enough to eke out a living. Even the poor-quality stuff gets put into drums and most of that is sold to China where people carve it into wonderful shapes—animals or vases, all kinds of things. The next grade up is jewellery—cheaper pieces with a bit of colour in stone that can be polished to a high shine. That goes to local cutters and polishers mostly, but is also sold in drums to Europe. The good stuff, though, the very best, brings fantastic money, so sometimes we were rich and sometimes we lived on beans and toast for months on end.'

'And now? Betsy-Ann said he was on a good seam—that's the good stuff, is it?'

'The best I've ever seen,' Annabelle said quietly, then she stood up off the couch and headed for the bedroom, returning with a bundle of rag held carefully in outstretched hands. She unwrapped the grubby cloth to reveal what looked like a very ordinary rock about the size of a football. Then she broke it open—it had apparently been cracked already—and showed it to Nick, handing him one of the pieces.

He stared in wonder at the colours—red so vivid it burnt his eyes, oranges, greens and blues flickering like flames inside the red.

'But that's beautiful,' he said, trying to make out all the colours he could see and work out how this piece of stone had created such magic in its heart.

'Dad had these holes in the hill, in the part that hadn't been blasted away. Every time he got on good opal, he'd put pieces in the holes for us—his girls—one hole for Betsy-Ann and Molly-May and one hole for Kitty and me. Sometimes he had to take the opal out to sell to buy some food or fix a piece of his equipment, but he'd always put something back in eventually, even if it wasn't top quality. I found this in our hole—in mine and Kitty's. I don't know if Betsy-Ann even knew about the holes, but if she's been out here while Dad was finding stones of this quality, she'll have made sure she got hold of some.'

Nick didn't want to ask what it was worth—surely something so beautiful would be priceless.

Had Annabelle read his thoughts that her next remark answered his query?

'It will pay Kitty's university fees and put a deposit

on a house for her, so she'll be all set up when she starts work.'

'And you?' Nick asked, aware by now that Annabelle showed more concern about her sister's future than she did about her own.

'I might stay out here. The drillers won't be here for ever and I don't know if the government will fund a nurse out here permanently, but in the immediate future it would save the mining company money if they only had to send a doctor and for a while I wouldn't need to be paid.'

'You'd give up your career in the ER, where you're a wonderful nurse, to stay out here to make sure Mrs Warren takes her heart pills?'

'And patch up accident victims, and see the patients who need regular checks, and stabilise patients who might need to be flown out. I could run well-patient clinics and take a counselling course to help people with anxiety—that's a huge problem in the country, especially among men. There'd be plenty to do and, really, Nick, the people out here deserve some stability in their medical assistance. Life's tough enough without having a new nurse and doctor every two months.'

'But you'd be cutting yourself off from life,' Nick protested.

'From what life?' Annabelle retorted. 'From movie theatres and wine bars and fancy eating places? They've never been high on my to-do list, and there's plenty of life out here—country folk make their own fun.'

'As I saw at the B and S ball,' Nick said in a tone so dry Annabelle flinched.

She had no idea why she'd got into this conversation with Nick, and now she wanted nothing more than to get out of it. She was exhausted, both physically and emotionally.

'Enough. I'm going to bed,' she said, shoving all the bits of paper back into the box and lifting it off the bed, wrapping the big rock of opal in the rag and putting it in on top.

'You need to eat,' Nick said, and this time she cringed because his voice was soft and gentle, as if he cared about the devastation she'd been through today.

Cared about her, perhaps…

Of course not—well, no more than as a colleague.

'I'll make some soup and toast. I won't be long.'

Too wiped out to argue, Annabelle found a clean nightshirt and headed for the bathroom again. Okay, so she was clean but out here the water was free, a gift from the earth, and standing again under a hot shower might release some of the pressure that had built up in her mind and body, and free her brain from the distracting thoughts that chased like tumbleweed through her head.

Soup was waiting for her, hot and delicious, produced so quickly Annabelle had to ask.

'Did Eileen leave this for us?'

Nick smirked.

'Hidden talents,' he replied. 'You know I can manage to scrape together a meal but soup's the easiest, especially this soup. Packet chicken noodle, a tin of creamed corn and swirl a couple of beaten eggs through it at the last minute—most of the major food groups covered in one bowl.'

Annabelle sat on the lounge and spooned soup into her mouth, taking bites of toast from time to time, suddenly aware she was very hungry, but even more aware of the depths of this man with whom she shared a house.

Before meeting him, she'd accepted the popular description of him, a man who was going places, but always in style. The Nick she'd got to know was as down-to-earth as anyone she'd ever met, practical, thoughtful, caring of all the patients he saw, and so supportive of her—a woman he barely knew. Just thinking about how kind he'd been today made her want to cry again.

Not that she would—she'd shed enough tears. It was time to look ahead, not behind, and although she'd told Nick the thoughts she'd had of staying on out here, she hadn't really considered it seriously.

Perhaps she should—consider it, that was. She knew that, feeling as she did about him, she couldn't work in close proximity to Nick, and if she was changing jobs, why not stay out here?

'Finish your soup while it's hot,' Nick told her, and she realised she'd stopped eating as her mind chased the possibility and her heart ached, though not this time for the loss of her father.

This time it ached for the loss of love.

Love?

Surely it wasn't love!

What did *she* know of love?

Annabelle finished the soup, washed her plate and bowl and spoon, said a polite thank-you to Nick and went to bed.

One day melded into the next, people brought flowers and casseroles, cards offering tribute to her father, and through it all Annabelle insisted on working, going stoically about her job, smiling politely, thanking people for their kindness, all but killing Nick who could see the pain she was hiding behind this professional façade.

'We'll take the splint off Max's hand and remove the stitches,' he said—professional talk was all they could manage as she'd distanced herself from him. Hiding behind a wall of grief, or something else. Nick didn't know, and that upset him too. 'It will be interesting to see how much movement he'll have in the finger.'

They were driving out to the drilling camp, Nick at the wheel, the new polite Annabelle not even arguing over who drove these days.

He stopped the car, put on the handbrake, and turned to her.

'Are you hating this as much as I am?' he demanded. 'And don't say "What, this?" in that innocent little voice of yours because you know damn well what I mean. I know you're grieving, Annabelle, and I know you have to cope with your grief as best you can, but this distant-colleague thing—is it because of what I said, because I was stupid enough to tell you that maybe how I felt was love?'

Dark eyes widened in surprise and she stared at him.

'You didn't say maybe what you felt was love, Nick,' she reminded him. 'You only said maybe it wasn't comfort. What was I to make of that?'

Frustration filled him, tightening his muscles and bamboozling his brain.

'You might have guessed,' he snapped.

'Guessed you loved me when you'd already told me you were done with love?'

'I didn't tell you I was done with love. I just told you it had let me down—women had let me down—but maybe

I was just as much to blame as them for mistaking the attraction I felt towards them for something deeper, calling it love because I didn't know another word for it.'

He paused, rubbing his hands over his face then threading his fingers through his floppy dark hair.

'Calling it love because I didn't know what love was,' he finally said, his voice so gruff Annabelle could barely make out the words.

But once she did work out what he'd said, she was in even more trouble, trying to decide what he meant by them.

'And now you do?' she said, hesitation stringing out the question. 'Now you understand?'

'Of course I do,' he snapped. 'I met you and my whole world turned upside down. Not immediately but as good as. Right from the plane trip I felt things I'd never felt before, and for a know-it-all woman who had no compunction in letting me know how ignorant I was about my own country.'

'You don't sound very happy about it,' Annabelle pointed out, although somewhere deep inside her the flower of hope was tentatively unfurling a petal.

'Well, I'm not. If anyone in the world deserves commitment and a wholehearted love, it's you, Annabelle, and my history makes me wonder if I can give you that. Oh, I'd want to, and be determined to, but what if I'm just not the kind of man women can stay in love with?'

Aware he'd just made a total idiot of himself, Nick gave a great sigh, put the vehicle into gear and pulled back onto the road.

'Listen to me,' he said, trying to make light of the awkward situation he'd created, 'talking about doom and gloom in the future when I've no idea if there could be

a future—no idea whether you feel anything at all for
me. I don't know what's happened to me, and you can
ignore the whole thing, but even if you don't want my
love, could we please go back to being friends?'

'I doubt that,' his passenger said eventually, then she
qualified it with, 'Though couldn't we be friends as well
as lovers?'

Nick stopped the car again, carefully put on the brake
and turned to her.

'Are you saying that you love me, or just suggesting
an affair?'

She smiled at him and reached out to take his hand,
turning it so she could trace a heart on his palm with
her forefinger.

'How could I not love you, Nick?' she whispered.
'You are the kindest, most compassionate man I've ever
met. You give so much of yourself to every patient, you
understand the pain of loss and heartbreak, you don't
pretend you know it all, but you make sure you learn to
do things properly, you put people at their ease no matter
what their problem.'

He ran the compliments through his head, sure something basic was missing in the conversation.

'You're going to say but there's love and love, aren't
you? You're going to tell me that for all these wonderful
attributes you've given me—definitely exaggerated—
you don't love me in a love and marriage way.'

She smiled now and his heart turned over in his chest,
or maybe it was his stomach that turned over—something moved for sure.

'I *do* love you that way,' she told him, 'or I think I
do—the same way you think you love me. But do we
really know each other? Can love really come to life in

such a short time—and if it can, would a love that happens so quickly disappear as quickly?'

Coldness filtered through his body.

He could understand where she was coming from, growing up and seeing women come and go through her father's life.

Could she be right?

No, he'd known Jill for months before they'd become engaged, although with Nellie barely a month had passed before they'd married, but whatever had happened in the past, some instinct told him this was different, and the same instinct insisted that if he let Annabelle go now, he would lose his love for ever.

He released the brake and drove on.

'Best we put love aside until we've got the clinic done,' he suggested.

'Well, you started the stupid conversation,' the woman he was pretty sure he loved snapped, and he had to smile. *That* was the Annabelle he knew!

And loved?

A helicopter they hadn't seen before was parked on the small pad beyond the main structures of the camp, and as Nick climbed out of the troopie, a man in suit trousers, white shirt and tie came out of the office.

'Nick!' he called, and Nick felt a wave of despair rush through him.

Not now, not yet! he wanted to yell, but the man kept coming, holding out his hand as he drew nearer.

'Charles!' Nick shook the offered hand then turned to Annabelle, who'd left the car and come round the front to stand close, but not too close, to him.

'Annabelle, this is Charles Gordon, head of Gordon

Oil and Gas, the company drilling out here. Charles, Annabelle Donne is the nurse on this placement.'

Nick watched the pair shake hands, Charles smiling warmly, telling Annabelle what a wonderful job the teams had been doing at Murrawalla and how much GOG appreciated it.

No fool, Annabel was looking from the smooth-talking city man to Nick, a thousand questions in her eyes.

She didn't have to wait long for answers. Charles was speaking again.

'I know you wanted more time out here to check out the arrangements, but things are happening faster than we thought. We should have the well sealed, the pump installed, and then it's just a matter of putting in pipe-lines to connect up with other lines we have in the area, then apart from occasional maintenance the operation here will be done.'

'Which means you'll no longer be funding a doctor and a nurse at Murrawalla?' Annabelle enquired, her voice as cold as the eyes that flashed their scorn at Nick.

'That's right,' Charles said cheerily, oblivious to the undercurrents swirling around him. 'I thought Nick would have told you.'

Scorn turned to hurt—to condemnation and betray-al—but Nick could hardly remind Charles he'd been warned to say nothing, and he couldn't explain to Annabelle, not here and now, that—

'But your idea—that report you sent, Nick, about what was really needed being permanent staff out here—well, that could work out.'

Nick didn't look at her, which was just as well because

Annabelle was flushed with shame that she'd thought so ill of him. Permanent staff—of course it was what the town needed—even if it was just a nurse. The population hardly justified a doctor as well.

'You see, we're thinking of a refining plant—not out here, it's too darned awkward, but closer to the town. It doesn't take much to clean up the oil and, *voilà*, you've got diesel. It's the fuel of choice in country areas and we can get it to people so much more cheaply if it's done here rather than running it all the way to a refinery in Brisbane then trucking it back.'

Annabelle felt an arm snake around her shoulders and although she tried to resist, Nick drew her close.

'If you're looking for a nurse and doctor team, can we apply?' he said to Charles.

'You'd stay here? You and Nurse Donne? Man, are you sure?'

'*Man, are you mad?* should have been the question, Mr Gordon,' Annabelle said. 'Now, if you'd excuse us for a moment, we've something to discuss and then a clinic to do.'

Charles Gordon nodded, and Annabelle, gripping the hand that had grasped her shoulder, tugged Nick back behind the troopie.

'Are you out of your mind? Offering to stay out here? What about the job as head of ER? Isn't that what you've been working towards all these years? Hasn't that always been your ambition? And what do you think you'll get paid as a doctor out here, for all the generosity of Mr Gordon? It'll be peanuts compared to what you could earn in the city.'

Nick leaned back against the troopie and smiled at the enraged woman in front of him.

'Finished?' he asked.

She glared at him, but had obviously run out of objections.

'You said yourself you were thinking of staying out here. Wouldn't it be your dream job? Do you think I haven't seen the longing in your eyes when you look out over the red desert country? Do you think I haven't heard your sighs as the sunset lights up your life or the stars stretch to infinity above you? As for me, yes, I'm a greenhorn, as the American cowboys would say, but I've never been in a place as strangely beautiful, and never felt such peace as when I stand with you to watch the sunset.'

She stared at him, then her mouth formed a little 'O' of wonder.

'You *do* love me,' she whispered. 'You must or you would never have known those things. But we don't have to stay out here, Nick. There's *your* life to consider.'

'My life is yours,' he said, and kissed the lips that were still trembling with uncertainty. 'Well, it will be when we've done the clinic…'

They walked together to the first-aid room, pleased to find only Max awaiting their attention. Most of the adhesive strips had worn off the back of his hand, and the scars were barely visible, while his finger, once the bandages and splint were removed, worked perfectly.

'It will be a little stiff for a while,' Nick warned him. 'Get hold of a tennis ball if you can and squeeze it for exercise.'

Max departed, leaving Nick and Annabelle alone.

Annabelle shook her head.

'This isn't really happening, is it? I've morphed into

something else and my avatar—isn't that what the game players have?—has taken over my life.'

'Let's see how the avatar handles kisses,' Nick suggested, and he took her in his arms and as his lips closed on hers, Annabelle felt a sense of rightness deep inside her.

Yes, she'd still find doubts, and argue them, both with herself and with Nick, but something deep inside felt as if she'd come home—not just physically to the country that she loved, but emotionally as well. In Nick she'd found her safe harbour, corny as she knew that sounded, and she snuggled closer to him, relishing the strength of his arms around her and the heat of his love on her lips.

# APRIL 2011
# HARDBACK TITLES

## ROMANCE

| | |
|---|---|
| Jess's Promise | Lynne Graham |
| Not For Sale | Sandra Marton |
| After Their Vows | Michelle Reid |
| A Spanish Awakening | Kim Lawrence |
| In Want of a Wife? | Cathy Williams |
| The Highest Stakes of All | Sara Craven |
| Marriage Made on Paper | Maisey Yates |
| Picture of Innocence | Jacqueline Baird |
| The Man She Loves To Hate | Kelly Hunter |
| The End of Faking It | Natalie Anderson |
| In the Australian Billionaire's Arms | Margaret Way |
| Abby and the Bachelor Cop | Marion Lennox |
| Misty and the Single Dad | Marion Lennox |
| Daycare Mum to Wife | Jennie Adams |
| The Road Not Taken | Jackie Braun |
| Shipwrecked With Mr Wrong | Nikki Logan |
| The Honourable Maverick | Alison Roberts |
| The Unsung Hero | Alison Roberts |

## HISTORICAL

| | |
|---|---|
| Secret Life of a Scandalous Debutante | Bronwyn Scott |
| One Illicit Night | Sophia James |
| The Governess and the Sheikh | Marguerite Kaye |
| Pirate's Daughter, Rebel Wife | June Francis |

## MEDICAL™

| | |
|---|---|
| Taming Dr Tempest | Meredith Webber |
| The Doctor and the Debutante | Anne Fraser |
| St Piran's: The Fireman and Nurse Loveday | Kate Hardy |
| From Brooding Boss to Adoring Dad | Dianne Drake |

0311 Gen Std LP

# APRIL 2011
# LARGE PRINT TITLES

## ROMANCE

| | |
|---|---|
| Naive Bride, Defiant Wife | Lynne Graham |
| Nicolo: The Powerful Sicilian | Sandra Marton |
| Stranded, Seduced...Pregnant | Kim Lawrence |
| Shock: One-Night Heir | Melanie Milburne |
| Mistletoe and the Lost Stiletto | Liz Fielding |
| Angel of Smoky Hollow | Barbara McMahon |
| Christmas at Candlebark Farm | Michelle Douglas |
| Rescued by his Christmas Angel | Cara Colter |

## HISTORICAL

| | |
|---|---|
| Innocent Courtesan to Adventurer's Bride | Louise Allen |
| Disgrace and Desire | Sarah Mallory |
| The Viking's Captive Princess | Michelle Styles |
| The Gamekeeper's Lady | Ann Lethbridge |

## MEDICAL™

| | |
|---|---|
| Bachelor of the Baby Ward | Meredith Webber |
| Fairytale on the Children's Ward | Meredith Webber |
| Playboy Under the Mistletoe | Joanna Neil |
| Officer, Surgeon...Gentleman! | Janice Lynn |
| Midwife in the Family Way | Fiona McArthur |
| Their Marriage Miracle | Sue MacKay |

**MAY 2011
HARDBACK TITLES**

# ROMANCE

| | |
|---|---|
| Too Proud to be Bought | Sharon Kendrick |
| A Dark Sicilian Secret | Jane Porter |
| Prince of Scandal | Annie West |
| The Beautiful Widow | Helen Brooks |
| Strangers in the Desert | Lynn Raye Harris |
| The Ultimate Risk | Chantelle Shaw |
| Sins of the Past | Elizabeth Power |
| A Night With Consequences | Margaret Mayo |
| Cupcakes and Killer Heels | Heidi Rice |
| Sex, Gossip and Rock & Roll | Nicola Marsh |
| Riches to Rags Bride | Myrna Mackenzie |
| Rancher's Twins: Mum Needed | Barbara Hannay |
| The Baby Project | Susan Meier |
| Second Chance Baby | Susan Meier |
| The Love Lottery | Shirley Jump |
| Her Moment in the Spotlight | Nina Harrington |
| Her Little Secret | Carol Marinelli |
| The Doctor's Damsel in Distress | Janice Lynn |

# HISTORICAL

| | |
|---|---|
| Lady Drusilla's Road to Ruin | Christine Merrill |
| Glory and the Rake | Deborah Simmons |
| To Marry a Matchmaker | Michelle Styles |
| The Mercenary's Bride | Terri Brisbin |

# MEDICAL™

| | |
|---|---|
| The Taming of Dr Alex Draycott | Joanna Neil |
| The Man Behind the Badge | Sharon Archer |
| St Piran's: Tiny Miracle Twins | Maggie Kingsley |
| Maverick in the ER | Jessica Matthews |

# MAY 2011
# LARGE PRINT TITLES

## ROMANCE

| | |
|---|---|
| Hidden Mistress, Public Wife | Emma Darcy |
| Jordan St Claire: Dark and Dangerous | Carole Mortimer |
| The Forbidden Innocent | Sharon Kendrick |
| Bound to the Greek | Kate Hewitt |
| Wealthy Australian, Secret Son | Margaret Way |
| A Winter Proposal | Lucy Gordon |
| His Diamond Bride | Lucy Gordon |
| Juggling Briefcase & Baby | Jessica Hart |

## HISTORICAL

| | |
|---|---|
| Courting Miss Vallois | Gail Whitiker |
| Reprobate Lord, Runaway Lady | Isabelle Goddard |
| The Bride Wore Scandal | Helen Dickson |
| Chivalrous Captain, Rebel Mistress | Diane Gaston |

## MEDICAL™

| | |
|---|---|
| Dr Zinetti's Snowkissed Bride | Sarah Morgan |
| The Christmas Baby Bump | Lynne Marshall |
| Christmas in Bluebell Cove | Abigail Gordon |
| The Village Nurse's Happy-Ever-After | Abigail Gordon |
| The Most Magical Gift of All | Fiona Lowe |
| Christmas Miracle: A Family | Dianne Drake |